MALACHI'S COVE

Anthony Trollope (1815–1882) combined his career as an important official in the Post Office with that of writing. In addition to forty-seven novels, he wrote many other works of biography, autobiography, travel and short stories, and was also a frequent contributor to periodicals. In 1868 he stood for Parliament but was defeated. In his own lifetime Trollope was recognised as one of the greatest novelists of his age. After his death his reputation suffered some decline but is now higher than ever.

Richard Mullen was born in the United States but has lived in England since 1969. After receiving a doctorate from the University of Oxford he taught both there and in the University of London. He has edited Mrs Frances Trollope's *Domestic Manners of the Americans* for Oxford University Press and is writing a biography of Anthony Trollope. He has also written for the B.B.C. and his programmes include the centenary tribute to Anthony Trollope and a feature on Frances Trollope's travels in America.

MALACHI'S COVE

and other Stories and Essays

ANTHONY TROLLOPE

Edited and with an Introduction by
RICHARD MULLEN

TABB HOUSE
Padstow, Cornwall

Published by Tabb House 1985
11 Church Street, Padstow, Cornwall, PL28 8 BG
in cased and limp editions

Introduction © Richard Mullen 1985

ISBN   0 907 018 35 1 Cased
ISBN   0 907 018 36 X Limp

Typeset by Inforum Ltd., Portsmouth
Printed and bound in England by
Robert Hartnoll Ltd., Bodmin

The Tabb House 'ENCORE' Series of Reprints

The Haunting
C. A. Dawson Scott
with a Foreword by Francis King

Malachi's Cove, and other Stories and Essays
Anthony Trollope
Edited and with an Introduction by Richard Mullen

One Poor Scruple
Mrs Wilfrid Ward
with an Introduction by Bernard Bergonzi

and other titles to follow

LIST OF CONTENTS

INTRODUCTION

Anthony Trollope is now recognised as one of the greatest and perhaps the most popular of Victorian novelists. Many of his forty-seven novels are widely read and appreciated today. Yet if his success as a novelist has been increasingly acclaimed, his achievements in other literary fields remain little known. Trollope produced an astonishing range of writing that no other major Victorian writer even attempted: novels, political history and comment, biography, travel books, translations from the classics, lectures, drama, art criticism and autobiography. In the course of his long literary career, Trollope wrote many short stories, or tales, most of which he later re-published in five volumes. In addition to the stories he also produced a large number of essays on a wide range of topics.

Trollope's short stories and essays have received comparatively little attention. This is regrettable, because of the inate quality of many of the stories and essays, as well as the light they reflect on his life. Anyone who wishes to understand Anthony Trollope should read his stories and essays. Without knowing them you do not know him, for they grew out of his life and travels. The stories are much more autobiographical than his novels and through them and his essays it is possible to follow Anthony Trollope's life as a writer.

Travelling and the writing of fiction proved to be an inseparable legacy for Trollope from his remarkable mother and these form the theme of this selection. Anthony Trollope was born in 1815, the youngest of Frances Trollope's four sons. By 1827, Fanny Trollope—as she was known—decided to travel to the American frontier. The reasons why she did this were a complex mixture arising from declining fortune and increased family tension. Her husband, a scholarly but irrational barrister, had abandoned the law to set up as a gentleman farmer; but he was already careening down the road to bankruptcy.

Fanny Trollope stayed in America for over three years and although her residence there was a series of disasters, she

produced on her return to England the most controversial, as
well as one of the best, travel books of the century: *Domestic
Manners of the Americans*.[1] Well over age fifty, she had found
in writing a way to support her family. The lesson was not lost
on Anthony even though he was the only member of the family
who did not spend some time in America with his mother.
Instead he was having a miserable time at Winchester and
Harrow.

After a youth of unrelieved failure and frustration, a place
was found for the young Trollope in the Post Office. For over
thirty years this official career gave a balance to Trollope's life.
His work also involved him in considerable world travel but
the Post Office provided a generous expense account with
which to enjoy it. Most of the stories in this collection are
connected with his work as a Post Office official. Although
they were all written and published in the 1860s, they reflect
aspects of his life over the preceding twenty years.

In 1841, at the age of 26, Trollope was sent to Ireland. Before
then his life had been "years of suffering, disgrace, and inward
remorse." "But from the day on which I set my foot in Ireland
all these evils went away from me. Since that time who has had
a happier life than mine?" Ireland provides the setting for
"Father Giles of Ballymoy." In his *Autobiography*, Trollope
says of this story "I will not swear to every detail . . . but the
main purport . . . is true." The story is set in the early months
of Trollope's life in Ireland.[2] Indeed, Trollope was to become
virtually unique amongst English writers of his time in knowing and liking Ireland. He would set his first two novels there as
well as his forty-seventh and final novel.

He was not blind to the flaws and faults of the people. In
"Father Giles" he alludes to one thing that continually infuri-
ated him: the large number of idle men he saw everywhere.
Idleness was the greatest vice to Trollope and, unlike many
denouncers of this particular sin, he practised what he preached.
"Father Giles" is also remarkable for the pains he took with the
Irish dialogue. Trollope was later to criticise his literary hero,
Thackeray, for not understanding the brogue of "dear County
Galway."[3] Trollope's rendition of Irish speech may not be

flawless, but he resists the temptation to portray the stage Irishman in his dialogue.

In this short story Trollope depicts a Catholic priest in a very favourable and charming light as one of the "best Christians" he had met. This was not a new development in his writing. From his first novel, *The Macdermots of Ballycloran* (1847), to one of his last, *An Eye for an Eye* (1879) Trollope depicts the Irish Catholic clergy with sympathy and warmth founded upon personal friendships. His religious venom was reserved for Evangelical clergymen like Mr Slope in *Barchester Towers* (1857). The Catholic *Dublin Review* praised him as being "keenly observant, painstaking, absolutely sincere and unprejudiced."[4]

Trollope won a good reputation with his Post Office superiors for his work in Ireland and was frequently asked to undertake special assignments. The first of these was to improve the delivery of the mails in the South West of England. This mission led to two considerable achievements: the introduction of the pillar-box and the creation of the Barsetshire novels, beginning with *The Warden* (1855). Trollope rode all over the South West enquiring about postal deliveries. Cornwall was one of the counties he saw "with a minuteness which few have enjoyed."[5] Cornwall in the early 1850s was quite isolated from the rest of the country: it truly was, as Wilkie Collins called it, "a land beyond railways." This sense of isolation is well portrayed in "Malachi's Cove."

Cornwall was seldom a setting for Trollope's stories or novels. He had introduced some Cornish mine workers into a scene in one novel, *The Three Clerks* (1857) and twenty years later he inserted some Cornish scenes in *The Duke's Children* (1880). But this novel lacks the vivid local colour that "Malachi's Cove" evokes.[6] It is, therefore, somewhat ironic that Trollope's writing is often said to lack a strong sense of place or description. "Malachi's Cove" shows that he is quite capable of depicting scenery when it is necessary. It is also said that Trollope was not very good at portraying common people. While this may have some validity in his novels—or at least his English novels—it is not the case with his short stories. Here again, "Malachi's Cove" is an excellent corrective.

By the late 1850s Trollope was being sent on foreign missions to negotiate postal treaties. "The Journey to Panama" is drawn from a trip in 1858–9 to the West Indies and Central America. It is interesting to see that he makes his heroine, if she can be so called, an Irishwoman and again, one with no shades of caricature. Trollope frequently depicts in his novels and stories the plight of women forced into marriage in an age when they had few other options. This is what he called in another short story, "An Unprotected Woman at the Pyramids", "the old-world idea that women, like green peas, cannot come to perfection without supporting-sticks." His fiction offers few more pathetic figures than Emily Viner, driven into a marriage: a ship is the perfect setting for such an endless journey to and from sadness. This story is one of the first classic ship-board tales that have been developed by such later masters of the form as F. Scott Fitzgerald and Somerset Maugham. This is just one way in which Trollope was a pioneer in short story writing. In *John Caldigate* (1879) Trollope himself developed the ship-board romance into something with sinister implications.

It is not known whether Trollope drew the actual plot from someone he observed aboard ship. We do know that the ship itself, which he calls the *Serrapiqui* (after a river in Costa Rica which he once explored in a canoe) is based on the *Atrato*, which carried him to St Thomas in 1858. That great Trollopian, Michael Sadleir, praises this story for being "courageously 'unfinished' " and says it is "vital to an understanding of his full-length work."[7]

After all his wanderings round the Caribbean Trollope felt in need of a rest. He went on holiday to the French Pyrenees for six weeks—the Civil Service provided long holidays in those halcyon days—with his wife Rose, his brother Thomas Adolphus and his brother-in-law, John Tilley, also a high Post Office official. While there Trollope wrote many short stories. "La Mère Bauche" reminds one more of Balzac than of Trollope. Life seems to be lived on a simpler and more tragic scale among these mountains than in the comfortable rectories and gracious mansions of Barset. The story of jilted love is a familiar one in Trollope, but none leads to such tragedy as this moving tale. Lily Dale in *Small House at Allington*, written a few years later, may be jilted by Adolphus Crosbie, but her tragedy does not equal that of Marie Clavert, abandoned by her Adolphe Bauche.

When Trollope returned from the Pyrenees he was plunged into a whirl-wind of novel writing at an incredible pace yet with astonishingly high quality. In the midst of this he embarked on yet another postal trip, this time to the United States, or at least to the northern part of the then dis-united States in the midst of a great Civil War. One reason Trollope wished to go was to emulate his mother and write a book about America. Although his *North America* lacks the verve of his mother's book, no other English writer of the century knew America as well as Trollope. He particularly liked Boston and spent much time there. He had already begun a great friendship with a young Boston girl of literary pretensions, Kate Field, and this only increased his understanding of American attitudes toward England.

His American trip led to many stories of which "Miss Ophelia Gledd", set in Boston, is the most charming. Ophelia's Gledd's dilemma lies in contemplating marriage into an English landed family and her character is therefore certainly not based on Kate Field. If "La Mère Bauche" has affinities with Balzac, "Miss Ophelia Gledd" has similarities with Henry James. Trollope was to return to the theme of transatlantic courtship in novels like *He Knew He Was Right* (1869) and *The Duke's Children* (1880), as well as several other short stories.

"Miss Ophelia Gledd" is notable for Trollope's question about what made a "lady". The role and nature of the "gentleman" is at the heart of many of his novels. In this American tale, he considers the other pillars of the Victorian social order. As in so many of his short stories he poses the question and lets us ponder and answer. He also contrasts English and American customs of courtship and proclaims that there is no "fixed rule of morality" about them but "right or wrong according to the usages of the country." Here we have another of his great strengths: his sense of genial fairness.

Anthony Trollope's versatility as a writer naturally drew him to essays as well as to short stories. His essays have been unduly neglected. One reason may be that some were published anonymously. Another reason, perhaps a more important one, is that most of them are in a wide variety of publications. He had a high opinion of the quality of Victorian periodicals: "How little do they know, who talk of the padding of our periodicals, how much of the best thought the nation produces is given to make up the cheap morsel of ephemeral literature."[8] Some of these essays are not very good, for instance those on English politics. These were all too often both inspired and destroyed by his passionate hatred of Disraeli.

Yet on other subjects, be they clergymen or London tradesmen, he can be an amusing and enlightening essayist. Perhaps his most interesting essays are those dealing with the writing of fiction. Trollope's article, "Charles Dickens" is an example both of his skill as an essayist and his own attitude towards the writing of novels. It was often thought at the time that Trollope took little interest in any fiction other than his own. One critic even alleged that "though he certainly took pleasure in writing novels, I doubt whether he took any in reading them . . . I should judge he had not read a dozen, even of Dickens."[9] This is pure nonsense. Even before writing any novels of his own, Trollope had read widely in fiction. It had been the hope of his frustrated youth to leap to fame with a scholarly history of literature and it was a project he turned to from time to time, though he never progressed very far in it.

Two literary giants dominated Victorian fiction: Thackeray and Dickens. Thackeray became Trollope's hero and friend, and he later wrote a book about Thackeray. Towards Dickens his feelings were more complex. He resented certain aspects of Dickens's writing: his constant attacks on government officials and what Trollope saw as his tendency toward caricature. Yet towards the man he felt an affection, which, if not as deep as that for Thackeray, was warm and genuine none the less. When Dickens was leaving America for the last time, Trollope was arriving on his third visit. Dickens's manager was struck at "the cordiality of the meeting of the two friends." Trollope and Dickens worked together for various charities and Dickens said of the younger novelist that no one in distress could have a "truer or stauncher friend."[10] Even so, Trollope always felt that Dickens ranked behind both Thackeray and George Eliot (another close friend of Trollope's) as a novelist. Trollope did not like Dickens's style: it was "jerky" and "ungrammatical" although ironically this was a charge frequently made against Trollope himself. But in the appreciation of Dickens included in this collection, Trollope writes warmly about his recently deceased friend.

The two themes of this collection—travel and fiction—are united in the second essay, "A Walk in a Wood". This is perhaps the most important essay Trollope ever wrote for anyone interested in understanding his writing. Here, in 1879, only three years before his death, he gives us an insight into how he thought about and wrote his novels. In "A Walk in the Wood" Trollope also talks about his walks in various parts of the world. He had travelled in all the places he mentions. Some of the later travels were to visit his younger son who had settled in Australia. There is a rather sad aspect to the passage where Trollope speaks of his hatred of the noise of brass bands. It is said that a fight with the leader of a German brass band brought on the fatal stroke which led to his death on December 6th, 1882.

II

Before reading the short stories and essays in this collection, it is helpful to know for whom they were written. Trollope was a highly professional author who was concerned to write at the right level for whatever audience he was addressing. This influenced all the pieces included here.

Trollope's greatest success was in the 1860's: the decade when all these stories were first published. As his success increased, editors and publishers began to seek him out for

contributions. One of these was the Revd Norman Macleod, a
Presbyterian minister who was Queen Victoria's favourite
preacher. Early in 1862, Macleod wrote as "the Editor of a
humble sixpenny monthly—*Good Words* . . . with the respect
and reverence becoming a beggar seeking crumbs from a rich
man's table." "You never perhaps heard of *Good Words*? . . .
Our circulation is now 70,000 . . . Name your price . . . you
and Kingsley are the only two men whom I should like to have
a story from—and I should feel proud to have you . . . in my
pages."[11] This flattering letter began a pleasant friendship for
Trollope and over the years he was to write many things for
Good Words, among which was "Malachi's Cove", published
in the magazine in December, 1864.

Some time before "Malachi's Cove" appeared, *Good Words*
had been attacked by a fanatical Evangelical newspaper, *The
Record*, for having "trashy tales" with "the most ungodly
sentiments". Trollope in particular, was singled out for his
involvement with the magazine, and he was, therefore, well
aware of how Macleod suffered from attacks of "ungodliness"
for daring to mix the sacred and the secular. Thus, in "Malachi's
Cove" he carefully informs the reader that Mally had become a
church-goer. Some might say that the small section about her
and the clergyman interrupts the flow of the story, but Trollope
knew both what his audience liked and what his editor needed.

The publisher of *Good Words* was Alexander Strahan. In
1866 he asked Trollope to write for another of his magazines,
The Argossy. "I do not know if you have ever seen *The
Argossy*" wrote Strahan in April, 1866. "Hitherto it has not
done well, but it must do well yet, for it is very good and very
cheap . . . let me ask you to give me a short sketch of, say, ten
to twelve pages and I will gladly pay you your own terms."[12]
Trollope evidently set to work quickly for "Father Giles of
Ballymoy" appeared in the next month's issue. Trollope
received £60 for the story. Both *The Argossy* and *Good
Words* were aimed at middle-class family audiences. They liked
a good simple tale with a basic plot and preferably some
moral message. There was no demand for the more subtle

analysis of character that distinguishes Trollope's best novels.

Trollope did not only write for money, as two of the short stories in this collection attest. He was a charitable man and was particularly kind to anyone involved with the production of books. He supported the efforts of Emily Faithfull to set up a firm of women printers. Trollope, along with many other leading authors, contributed works to her books without asking for any payment. Emily Faithfull published a lavish volume in 1861 called *Victoria Regia*, which was dedicated to the Queen. The purpose was to raise money to help her women printers. "The Journey to Panama" first appeared here. Its theme, the plight of a woman without money, forced to seek a refuge in an arranged marriage, was an appropriate one for Emily Faithfull. A few years later she produced yet another luxurious book called *A Welcome* which consisted of articles by many writers to celebrate the marriage of the Prince of Wales to the beautiful Princess Alexandra of Denmark. "Miss Ophelia Gledd" was Trollope's gift to this book; again the theme of a foreign girl marrying an Englishman is appropriate. Both of these stories were intended for a wealthier and more sophisticated audience than those who read *Good Words* or *The Argosy*. Hence the two stories pose deeper questions— that are not answered in either of them.

"La Mère Bauche" was written for *Harper's New Monthly Magazine* in New York. Trollope had paid a hurried visit to the firm on his way home from the West Indies in 1859. They agreed to publish various short stories by him and brought out "The Courtship of Susan Bell", a delightful love story set in America. However, although they had accepted and paid for "La Mère Bauche" they did not publish it in their magazine. Perhaps the foreign setting seemed too exotic, particularly as the United States was soon embroiled in its own troubles. Anthony Trollope, however, at least had the satisfaction to be amongst the first English authors to sell his stories directly to an American publisher. We do not know if Trollope changed the story for an English audience when he included it in *Lotta Schmidt*, one of the five volumes of short stories he later

published. It is probable that he did so as there are no specific-
ally American references.

The essay on Charles Dickens included in this selection was
published in *St Paul's Magazine*, which Trollope himself
edited and which he intended as a more serious and intellectual
journal than something like *The Argossy*.[13] His tribute to
Dickens is amongst the last pieces he wrote before leaving the
magazine. After he had given up the editorship of *St Paul's
Magazine*, Trollope was totally dependant on his fertile pen to
maintain his comfortable way of life, for he had already resigned
from the Post Office. He continued to write an incredible
amount of novels and other works. The final work in this
selection, "A Walk in a Wood" was written for *Good Words* in
1879. It was originally designed to be part of a series called
"Half Hours in the Fresh Air." After it was decided to publish
it on its own in *Good Words*, there was some debate about the
title. Trollope suggested calling it "How we write our books".
"It must not be more personal than that" he insisted. Ironically,
if it had been given Trollope's own title it would have received
the attention it richly deserves.

III

Finally, it is worth considering Anthony Trollope's place as a
writer of short stories. His stories are of an uneven quality,
perhaps more so than are his novels. The amount that he wrote
and the pace at which he wrote made this inevitable. The stories
in this collection are certainly among his best and they are
among the best of all Victorian short stories.

The short story in England was essentially a Victorian
creation. One can, of course, cite earlier examples, but as
Walter Allen puts it in *The Short Story in English*, the modern
short story was "invented" by Sir Walter Scott. Anthony
Trollope was twelve when, in 1827, Scott wrote "The Two
Drovers", which set the pattern for so much short story
writing. The short story was, therefore, a form of writing in

which Trollope had fewer examples to follow than he did with his novels or his essays. To some degree, then, Trollope was exploring new territory when he began writing short stories, just as he did in his Post Office career when he laid out mail routes.

Although the short story in England did not reach the artistic heights it did in the France of Flaubert and Maupassant or, for that matter, the America of Poe and Hawthorne, the genre was much advanced by the end of Trollope's life. Anthony Trollope could claim considerable credit for improving and popularising it. No other major Victorian novelist wrote so many tales (as he often called them) or published so many collected editions of them.

One reason why the short story made such advances was the tremendous growth of magazines in the period. The grander magazines preferred a serial novel while the great quarterlies disdained fiction in any form; but scores of other magazines sensed a growing market for stories. A professional author like Trollope was not one to neglect such a promising opportunity. His example was followed by many later writers.

It might be thought that a novelist like Trollope, well known for his skill in characterisation and his small regard for plot, would not be a good short story writer. As Robert Taylor so aptly puts it: "His method, style and indeed his whole theory of fiction were well suited by a loose rambling plot which left the characters free to develop and disport themselves as they chose."[14] Some contemporary critics, such as *The Spectator*, felt that the problem with Trollope's short stories was that they lacked "the first condition of Mr Trollope's success as a novelist—due length of narrative."[15] Now, well over a century after they first appeared, we can see that these stories are enjoyable and worthwhile because of their brevity. In the smaller compass we can often see Trollope better than in the three volume version.

The short stories are different from the novels in many ways. The language tends to be simpler, with fewer classical allusions. He also frequently writes in the first person, which adds to the immediacy of the story; only one novel after his first one is told in the first person. The short stories are also approached from a different perspective. They are often the stories of poor or tragic people. All the stories in this collection feature a main character who somehow differs from the world in which he lives, who is in some sense alienated: the poor working girl in Cornwall, the English official in rural Ireland, the orphan girl in France, the impoverished lady at sea and the American girl contemplating an English marriage. Trollope himself, in spite of his success in several careers, always retained something of the unhappy and isolated schoolboy in his character. This helped him to see and to write about other people's predicaments. The short stories present the compassionate Trollope looking at the people the Victorian world, like our own, often preferred to forget.

The collection assembled here begins to show the range and quality of Trollope's shorter works. Anyone already devoted to Trollope will be pleased to have more of his work available. To any new reader these stories and essays make an excellent and enjoyable introduction to the work of a very great writer and a delightful companion.

June, 1984   Richard Mullen
                                                          Oxford

NOTES

1. For Frances Trollope's American experiences see my forth-coming edition for Oxford University Press of her *Domestic Manners of the Americans*.

2. Anthony Trollope, *An Autobiography* (1950), pp. 60–63. (Unless noted otherwise, all books cited were published in London.)

3. Anthony Trollope, *Thackeray* (1902), pp. 174–5.

4. Anon., "The Novels of Mr Anthony Trollope" in *Dublin Review* (October, 1872), quoted in Donald Smalley (ed), *Anthony Trollope: The Critical Heritage* (1969), p.365.

5. *Autobiography*, p. 88

6. In July, 1876, Trollope replied to a letter from a bibliographer of Cornwall with information about "Malachi's Cove", saying it was set "somewhere on its coast." This was at the time he was writing *The Duke's Children*. Thus the recollection of "Malachi's Cove" may have influenced the Cornish scenes in *The Duke's Children*. See N. John Hall (ed), *The Letters of Anthony Trollope* (Stanford, California, 1983, 2 vols.), II. 695.

7. Michael Sadleir, *Trollope: A Commentary* (1927), p. 177.

8. Anthony Trollope, "George H. Lewes" in *Fortnightly Review* (January, 1879), p. 17.

9. James Payn, "Some Literary Recollections" in *Cornhill Magazine* (January, 1884), p. 53.

10. George Dolby, *Charles Dickens as I Knew Him* (1885), p. 325; Dickens to Trollope, 9 May, 1867 in the Parrish Collection, Princeton University Library, AM 15542. See also Anthony Trollope, "Novel Reading . . ." in *Nineteenth Century* (January, 1879).

11. Trollope Business Papers, Bodleian Library, Oxford, M.S. Don. c. 9–10*.

12. 3 April, 1866: Trollope Business Papers, Bodleian Library, Oxford.

13. See John Sutherland, "Trollope and *St Paul's*, 1866–70" in Tony Bareham (ed), *Anthony Trollope* (1980), pp. 116–37. Strahan was also involved in *St Paul's*.

14. Robert H. Taylor, *Certain Small Works* (Princeton, New Jersey, 1980), p. 102.

15. *Spectator*, 21 Sept. 1867. In this review of *Lotta Schmidt*, "Miss Ophelia Gledd" was particularly praised as "very striking". This anonymous review was probably by R. H. Hutton, Trollope's most perceptive reviewer.

Malachi's Cove

On the northern coast of Cornwall, between Tintagel and
Bossiney, down on the very margin of the sea, there lived not
long since[1] an old man who got his living by saving sea-weed
from the waves, and selling it for manure. The cliffs there are
bold and fine, and the sea beats in upon them from the north
with a grand violence. I doubt whether it be not the finest
morsel of cliff scenery in England, though it is beaten by many
portions of the west coast of Ireland, and perhaps also by spots
in Wales and Scotland. Cliffs should be nearly precipitous,
they should be broken in their outlines, and should barely
admit here and there of an insecure passage from their summit
to the sand at their feet. The sea should come, if not up to them,
at least very near to them, and then, above all things, the water
below them should be blue, and not of that dead leaden colour
which is so familiar to us in England. At Tintagel all these
requisites are there, except that bright blue colour which is so
lovely. But the cliffs themselves are bold and well broken, and
the margin of sand at high water is very narrow,—so narrow
that at spring-tides there is barely a footing there.

Close upon this margin was the cottage or hovel of Malachi
Trenglos, the old man of whom I have spoken. But Malachi, or
old Glos, as he was commonly called by the people around
him, had not built his house absolutely upon the sand. There
was a fissure in the rock so great that at the top it formed a
narrow ravine, and so complete from the summit to the base
that it afforded an opening for a steep and rugged track from
the top of the rock to the bottom. This fissure was so wide at
the bottom that it had afforded space for Trenglos to fix his
habitation on a foundation of rock, and here he had lived for
many years. It was told of him that in the early days of his trade
he had always carried the weed in a basket on his back to the
top, but latterly he had been possessed of a donkey which had
been trained to go up and down the steep track with a single
pannier over his loins, for the rocks would not admit of
panniers hanging by his side; and for this assistant he had built a

shed adjoining his own, and almost as large as that in which he himself resided.

But, as years went on, old Glos procured other assistance than that of the donkey, or, as I should rather say, Providence supplied him with other help; and, indeed, had it not been so, the old man must have given up his cabin and his independence and gone into the workhouse at Camelford. For rheumatism had afflicted him, old age had bowed him till he was nearly double, and by degrees he became unable to attend the donkey on its upward passage to the world above, or even to assist in rescuing the coveted weed from the waves.

At the time to which our story refers Trenglos had not been up the cliff for twelve months, and for the last six months he had done nothing towards the furtherance of his trade, except to take the money and keep it, if any of it was kept, and occasionally to shake down a bundle of fodder for the donkey. The real work of the business was done altogether by Mahala Trenglos, his granddaughter.

Mally Trenglos was known to all the farmers round the coast, and to all the small tradespeople in Camelford. She was a wild-looking, almost unearthly creature, with wild-flowing, black, uncombed hair, small in stature, with small hands and bright black eyes; but people said that she was very strong, and the children around declared that she worked day and night, and knew nothing of fatigue. As to her age there were many doubts. Some said she was ten, and others five-and-twenty, but the reader may be allowed to know that at this time she had in truth passed her twentieth birthday. The old people spoke well of Mally, because she was so good to her grandfather; and it was said of her that though she carried to him a little gin and tobacco almost daily, she bought nothing for herself;—and as to the gin, no one who looked at her would accuse her of meddling with that. But she had no friends, and but few acquaintances among people of her own age. They said that she was fierce and ill-natured, that she had not a good word for any one, and that she was, complete at all points, a thorough little vixen. The young men did not care for her; for, as regarded dress, all days were alike with her. She never made herself smart on Sundays. She was generally without stockings, and seemed to care not at all to exercise any of those feminine attractions which might have been hers had she studied to attain them. All days were the same to her in regard to dress; and, indeed, till lately, all days had, I fear, been the same to her in other respects. Old Malachi had never been seen inside a place of worship since he had taken to live under the cliff.

But within the last two years Mally had submitted herself to the teaching of the clergyman at Tintagel, and had appeared at church on Sundays, if not absolutely with punctuality, at any rate so often that no one who knew the peculiarity of her residence was disposed to quarrel with her on that subject. But she made no difference in her dress on these occasions. She took her place on a low stone seat just inside the church door, clothed as usual in her thick red serge petticoat and loose brown serge jacket, such being the apparel which she had found to be best adapted for her hard and perilous work among the waters. She had pleaded to the clergyman when he attacked her on the subject of church attendance with vigour that she had got no church-going clothes. He had explained to her that she would be received there without distinction to her clothing. Mally had taken him at his word, and had gone, with a courage which certainly deserved admiration, though I doubt whether there was not mingled with it an obstinacy which was less admirable.

For people said that old Glos was rich, and that Mally might have proper clothes if she chose to buy them. Mr. Polwarth, the clergyman, who, as the old man could not come to him, went down the rocks to the old man, did make some hint on the matter in Mally's absence. But old Glos, who had been patient with him on other matters, turned upon him so angrily when he made an allusion to money, that Mr. Polwarth found himself obliged to give that matter up, and Mally continued to sit upon the stone bench in her short serge petticoat, with her long hair streaming down her face. She did so far sacrifice to decency as on such occasions to tie up her black hair with an old shoe-string. So tied it would remain through the Monday and Tuesday, but by Wednesday afternoon Mally's hair had generally managed to escape.

As to Mally's indefatigable industry there could be no manner of doubt, for the quantity of seaweed which she and the donkey amassed between them was very surprising. Old Glos, it was declared, had never collected half what Mally gathered together; but then the article was becoming cheaper, and it was necessary that the exertion should be greater. So Mally and the donkey toiled and toiled, and the seaweed came up in heaps which surprised those who looked at her little hands and light form. Was there not some one who helped her at nights, some fairy, or demon, or the like? Mally was so snappish in her answers to people that she had no right to be surprised if ill-natured things were said of her.

No one ever heard Mally Trenglos complain of her work, but about this time she was heard to make great and loud complaints of the treatment she received from some of her neighbours. It was known that she went with her plaints to Mr. Polwarth; and when he could not help her, or did not give her such instant help as she needed, she went—ah, so foolishly! to the office of a certain attorney at Camelford, who was not likely to prove himself a better friend than Mr. Polwarth.

Now the nature of her injury was as follows. The place in which she collected her seaweed was a little cove; the people had come to call it Malachi's Cove from the name of the old man who lived there;—which was so formed, that the margin of the sea therein could only be reached by the passage from the top down to Trenglos's hut. The breadth of the cove when the sea was out might perhaps be two hundred yards, and on each side the rocks ran out in such a way that both from north and south the domain of Trenglos was guarded from intruders. And this locality had been well chosen for its intended purpose.

There was a rush of the sea into the cover, which carried there large, drifting masses of seaweed, leaving them among the rocks when the tide was out. During the equinoctial winds of the spring and autumn the supply would never fail; and even when the sea was calm, the long, soft, salt-bedewed, trailing masses of the weed, could be gathered there when they could not be found elsewhere for miles along the coast. The task of getting the weed from the breakers was often difficult and dangerous,—so difficult that much of it was left to be carried away by the next incoming tide.

Mally doubtless did not gather half the crop that was there at her feet. What was taken by the returning waves she did not regret; but when interlopers came upon her cove, and gathered her wealth,—her grandfather's wealth, beneath her eyes, then her heart was broken. It was this interloping, this intrusion, that drove poor Mally to the Camelford attorney. But, alas, though the Camelford attorney took Mally's money, he could do nothing for her, and her heart was broken!

She had an idea, in which no doubt her grandfather shared, that the path to the cove was, at any rate, their property. When she was told that the cove, and sea running into the cove, were not the freeholds of her grandfather, she understood that the statement might be true. But what then as to the use of the path? Who had made the path what it was? Had she not painfully, wearily, with exceeding toil, carried up bits of rock with her own little hands, that her grandfather's donkey might have footing for his feet? Had she not scraped together crumbs of earth along the face of the cliff that she might make easier to the animal the track of that rugged way? And now, when she saw big farmers' lads coming down with other donkeys,—and, indeed, there was one who came with a pony; no boy, but a young man, old enough to know better than rob a poor old man and a young girl,—she reviled the whole human race, and swore that the Camelford attorney was a fool.

Any attempt to explain to her that there was still weed enough for her was worse than useless. Was it not all hers and his, or, at any rate, was not the sole way to it his and hers? And was not her trade stopped and impeded? Had she not been forced to back her laden donkey down, twenty yards she said, but it had, in truth, been five, because Farmer Gunliffe's son had been in the way with his thieving pony? Farmer Gunliffe had wanted to buy her weed at his own price, and because she had refused he had set on his thieving son to destroy her in this wicked way.

"I'll hamstring the beast the next time as he's down here!"

said Mally to old Glos, while the angry fire literally streamed from her eyes.

Farmer Gunliffe's small homestead—he held about fifty acres of land—was close by the village of Tintagel, and not a mile from the cliff. The sea-wrack, as they call it, was pretty well the only manure within his reach, and no doubt he thought it hard that he should be kept from using it by Mally Trenglos and her obstinacy.

"There's heaps of other coves, Barty," said Mally to Barty Gunliffe, the farmer's son.

"But none so nigh, Mally, nor yet none that fills 'emselves as this place."

Then he explained to her that he would not take the weed that came up close to hand. He was bigger than she was, and stronger, and would get it from the outer rocks, with which she never meddled. Then, with scorn in her eye, she swore that she could get it where he durst not venture, and repeated her threat of hamstringing the pony. Barty laughed at her wrath, jeered her because of her wild hair, and called her a mermaid.

"I'll mermaid you!" she cried. "Mermaid, indeed! I wouldn't be a man to come and rob a poor girl and an old cripple. But you're no man, Barty Gunliffe! You're not half a man."

Nevertheless, Bartholomew Gunliffe was a very fine young fellow, as far as the eye went. He was about five feet eight inches high, with strong arms and legs, with light curly brown hair and blue eyes. His father was but in a small way as a farmer, but, nevertheless, Barty Gunliffe was well thought of among the girls around. Everybody liked Barty,— excepting only Mally Trenglos, and she hated him like poison.

Barty, when he was asked why so good-natured a lad as he persecuted a poor girl and an old man, threw himself upon the justice of the thing. It wouldn't do at all, according to his view, that any single person should take upon himself to own that which God Almighty sent as the common property of all. He would do Mally no harm, and so he had told her. But Mally was a vixen,—a wicked little vixen; and she must be taught to have a civil tongue in her head. When once Mally would speak him civil as he went for weed, he would get his father to pay the old man some sort of toll for the use of the path.

"Speak him civil?" said Mally. "Never; not while I have a tongue in my mouth!" And I fear old Glos encouraged her rather than otherwise in her view of the matter.

But her grandfather did not encourage her to hamstring the pony. Hamstringing a pony would be a serious thing, and old Glos thought it might be very awkward for both of them if Mally were put into prison. He suggested, therefore, that all manner of impediments should be put in the way of the pony's feet, surmising that the well-trained donkey might be able to work in spite of them. And Barty Gunliffe, on his next descent, did find the passage very awkward when he came near to Malachi's hut, but he made his way down, and poor Mally saw the lumps of rock at which she had laboured so hard pushed on one side or rolled out of the way with a steady persistency of injury towards herself that almost drove her frantic.

"Well, Barty, you're a nice boy," said old Glos, sitting in the doorway of the hut, as he watched the intruder.

"I ain't a doing no harm to none as doesn't harm me," said Barty. "The sea's free to all, Malachi."

"And the sky's free to all, but I mustn't get up on the top of your big barn to look at it," said Mally, who was standing among the rocks with a long hook in her hand. The long hook was the tool with which she worked in dragging the weed from the waves. "But you ain't got no justice nor yet no sperrit, or you wouldn't come here to vex an old man like he."

"I didn't want to vex him, nor yet to vex you, Mally. You let me be for a while, and we'll be friends yet."

"Friends!" exclaimed Mally. "Who'd have the likes of you for a friend? What are you moving them stones for? Them stones belongs to grandfather." And in her wrath she made a movement as though she were going to fly at him.

"Let him be, Mally," said the old man; "let him be. He'll get his punishment. He'll come to be drowned some day if he comes down here when the wind is in shore."

"That he may be drowned then!" said Mally, in her anger. "If he was in the big hole there among the rocks, and the sea running in at half tide, I wouldn't lift a hand to help him out."

"Yes, you would, Mally; you'd fish me up with your hook like a big stick of seaweed."

She turned from him with scorn as he said this, and went into the hut. It was time for her to get ready for her work, and one of the great injuries done her lay in this,—that such a one as Barty Gunliffe should come and look at her during her toil among the breakers.

It was an afternoon in April, and the hour was something after four o'clock. There had been a heavy wind from the north-west all the morning, with gusts of rain, and the sea-gulls had been in and out of the cove all the day, which was a sure sign to Mally that the incoming tide would cover the rocks with weed.

The quick waves were now returning with wonderful celerity over the low reefs, and the time had come at which the treasure must be seized, if it was to be garnered on that day. By seven o'clock it would be growing dark, at nine it would be high water, and before daylight the crop would be carried out again if not collected. All this Mally understood very well, and some of this Barty was beginning to understand also.

As Mally came down with her bare feet, bearing her long hook in her hand, she saw Barty's pony standing patiently on the sand, and in her heart she longed to attack the brute. Barty at this moment, with a common three-pronged fork in his hand, was standing down on a large rock, gazing forth towards the waters. He had declared that he would gather the weed only at places which were inaccessible to Mally, and he was looking out that he might settle where he would begin.

"Let 'un be, let 'un be," shouted the old man to Mally, as he saw her take a step towards the beast, which she hated almost as much as she hated the man.

Hearing her grandfather's voice through the wind, she desisted from her purpose, if any purpose she had had, and went forth to her work. As she passed down the cove, and scrambled in among the rocks, she saw Barty still standing on his perch; out beyond, the white-curling waves were cresting and breaking themselves with violence, and the wind was howling among the caverns and abutments of the cliff.

Every now and then there came a squall of rain, and though there was sufficient light, the heavens were black with clouds. A scene more beautiful might hardly be found by those who love the glories of the coast. The light for such objects was perfect. Nothing could exceed the grandeur of the colours,—the blue of the open sea, the white of the breaking waves, the yellow sands, or the streaks of red and brown which gave such richness to the cliff.

But neither Mally nor Barty were thinking of such things as these. Indeed they were hardly thinking of their trade after its ordinary forms. Barty was meditating how he might best accomplish his purpose of working beyond the reach of Mally's feminine powers, and Mally was resolving that wherever Barty went she would go farther.

And, in many respects, Mally had the advantage. She knew every rock in the spot, and was sure of those which gave a good foothold, and sure also of those which did not. And then her activity had been made perfect by practice for the purpose to which it was to be devoted. Barty, no doubt, was stronger than she, and quite as active. But Barty could not jump among the waves from one stone to another as she could do, nor was he as yet able to get aid in his work from the very force of the water as she could get it. She had been hunting seaweed in that cove since she had been an urchin of six years old, and she knew every hole and corner and every spot of vantage. The waves were her friends, and she could use them. She could measure their strength, and knew when and where it would cease.

Mally was great down in the salt pools of her own cove,—great, and very fearless. As she watched Barty make his way forward from rock to rock, she told herself, gleefully, that he was going astray. The curl of the wind as it blew into the cover would not carry the weed up to the northern buttresses of the cove; and then there was the great hole just there,—the great hole of which she had spoken when she wished him evil.

And now she went to work, hooking up the dishevelled hairs of the ocean, and landing many a cargo on the extreme margin of the sand, from whence she would be able in the evening to drag it back before the invading waters would return to reclaim the spoil.

And on his side also Barty made his heap up against the northern buttresses of which I have spoken. Barty's heap became big and still bigger, so that he knew, let the pony work as he might, he could not take it all up that evening. But still it was not as large as Mally's heap. Mally's hook was better than his fork, and Mally's skill was better than his strength. And when he failed in some haul Mally would jeer him with a wild, weird laughter, and shriek to him through the wind that he was not half a man. At first he answered her with laughing words, but before long, as she boasted of her success and pointed to his failure, he became angry, and then he answered her no more. He became angry with himself, in that he missed so much of the plunder before him.

The broken sea was full of the long straggling growth which the waves had torn up from the bottom of the ocean, but the masses were carried past him, away from him,—nay, once or twice over him; and then Mally's weird voice would sound in his ear, jeering him. The gloom among the rocks was now becoming thicker and thicker, the tide was beating in with increased strength, and the gusts of wind came with quicker and greater violence. But still he worked on. While Mally worked he would work, and he would work for some time after she was driven in. He would not be beaten by a girl.

The great hole was now full of water, but of water which seemed to be boiling as though in a pot. And the pot was full of floating masses,—large treasures of seaweed which were thrown to and fro upon its surface, but lying there so thick that one would seem almost able to rest upon it without sinking.

Mally knew well how useless it was to attempt to rescue aught from the fury of that boiling cauldron. The hole went in under the rocks, and the side of it towards the shore lay high, slippery, and steep. The hole, even at low water, was never empty; and Mally believed that there was no bottom to it. Fish thrown in there could escape out to the ocean, miles away,—so Mally in her softer moods would tell the visitors to the cove. She knew the hole well. Poulnadioul she was accustomed to call it; which was supposed, when translated, to mean that this was the hole of the Evil One. Never did Mally attempt to make her own of weed which had found its way into that pot.

But Barty Gunliffe knew no better, and she watched him as he endeavoured to steady himself on the treacherously slippery edge of the pool. He fixed himself there and made a haul, with some small success. How he managed it she hardly knew, but she stood still for a while watching him anxiously, and then she saw him slip. He slipped, and recovered himself;—slipped again, and again recovered himself.

"Barty, you fool!" she screamed; "if you get yourself pitched in there, you'll never come out no more."

Whether she simply wished to frighten him, or whether her heart relented and she had thought of his danger with dismay, who shall say? She could not have told herself. She hated him as much as ever,—but she could hardly have wished to see him drowned before her eyes.

"You go on, and don't mind me," said he, speaking in a hoarse, angry tone.

"Mind you!—who minds you?" retorted the girl. And then she again prepared herself for her work.

But as she went down over the rocks with her long hook balanced in her hands, she suddenly heard a splash, and turning quickly round, saw the body of her enemy tumbling amidst the eddying waves in the pool. The tide had now come up so far that every succeeding wave washed into it and over it from the side nearest to the sea, and then ran down again back from the rocks, as the rolling wave receded, with a noise like the fall of a cataract. And then, when the surplus water had retreated for a moment, the surface of the pool would be partly calm, though the fretting bubbles would still boil up and down, and there was ever a simmer on the surface, as though, in truth, the cauldron were heated. But this time of comparative rest was but a moment, for the succeeding breaker would come up almost as soon as the foam of the preceding one had gone, and then again the waters would be dashed upon the rocks, and the sides would echo with the roar of the angry wave.

Instantly Mally hurried across to the edge of the pool,

crouching down upon her hands and knees for security as she did so. As a wave receded, Barty's head and face was carried round near to her, and she could see that his forehead was covered with blood. Whether he were alive or dead she did not know. She had seen nothing but his blood, and the light-coloured hair of his head lying amidst the foam. Then his body was drawn along by the suction of the retreating wave; but the mass of water that escaped was not on this occasion large enough to carry the man out with it.

Instantly Mally was at work with her hook, and getting it fixed into his coat, dragged him towards the spot on which she was kneeling. During the half minute of repose she got him so close that she could touch his shoulder. Straining herself down, laying herself over the long bending handle of the hook, she strove to grasp him with her right hand. But she could not do it; she could only touch him.

Then came the next breaker, forcing itself on with a roar, looking to Mally as though it must certainly knock her from her resting-place, and destroy them both. But she had nothing for it but to kneel, and hold by her hook.

What prayer passed through her mind at that moment for herself or for him, or for that old man who was sitting unconsciously up at the cabin, who can say? The great wave came and rushed over her as she lay almost prostrate, and when the water was gone from her eyes, and the tumult of the foam, and the violence of the roaring breaker had passed by her, she found herself at her length upon the rock, while his body had been lifted up, free from her hook, and was lying upon the slippery ledge, half in the water and half out of it. As she looked at him, in that instant, she could see that his eyes were open and that he was struggling with his hands.

"Hold by the hook, Barty," she cried, pushing the stick of it before him, while she seized the collar of his coat in her hands.

Had he been her brother, her lover, her father, she could not have clung to him with more of the energy of despair. He did contrive to hold by the stick which she had given him, and when the succeeding wave had passed by, he was still on the ledge. In the next moment she was seated a yard or two above the hole, in comparative safety, while Barty lay upon the rocks with his still bleeding head resting upon her lap.

What could she do now? She could not carry him; and in fifteen minutes the sea would be up where she was sitting. He was quite insensible and very pale, and the blood was coming slowly,—very slowly,—from the wound on his forehead. Ever so gently she put her hand upon his hair to move it back from his face; and then she bent over his mouth to see if he breathed, and as she looked at him she knew that he was beautiful.

What would she not give that he might live? Nothing now was so precious to her as his life,—as this life which she had so far rescued from the waters. But what could she do? Her grandfather could scarcely get himself down over the rocks, if indeed he could succeed in doing so much as that. Could she drag the wounded man backwards, if it were only a few feet, so that he might lie above the reach of the waves till further assistance could be procured?

She set herself to work and she moved him, almost lifting him. As she did so she wondered at her own strength, but she was very strong at that moment. Slowly, tenderly, falling on the rocks herself so that he might fall on her, she got him back to the margin of the sand, to a spot which the waters would not reach for the next two hours.

Here her grandfather met them, having seen at last what had happened from the door.

"Dada," she said, "he fell into the pool yonder, and was battered against the rocks. See there at his forehead."

"Mally, I'm thinking that he's dead already," said old Glos, peering down over the body.

"No, dada; he is not dead; but mayhap he's dying. But I'll go at once up to the farm."

"Mally," said the old man, "look at his head. They'll say we murdered him."

"Who'll say so? Who'll lie like that? Didn't I pull him out of the hole?"

"What matters that? His father'll say we killed him."

It was manifest to Mally that whatever any one might say hereafter, her present course was plain before her. She must run up the path to Gunliffe's farm and get necessary assistance. If the world were as bad as her grandfather said, it would be so bad that she would not care to live longer in it. But be that as it might, there was no doubt as to what she must do now.

So away she went as fast as her naked feet could carry her up the cliff. When at the top she looked round to see if any person might be within ken, but she saw no one. So she ran with all her speed along the headland of the corn-field which led in the direction of old Gunliffe's house, and as she drew near to the homestead she saw that Barty's mother was leaning on the gate. As she approached, she attempted to call, but her breath failed her for any purpose of loud speech, so she ran on till she was able to grasp Mrs. Gunliffe by the arm.

"Where's himself?" she said, holding her hand upon her beating heart that she might husband her breath.

"Who is it you mean?" said Mrs Gunliffe, who participated in the family feud against Trenglos and his granddaughter. "What does the girl clutch me for in that way?"

"He's dying then, that's all."

"Who is dying? Is it old Malachi? If the old man's bad, we'll send some one down."

"It ain't dada, it's Barty! Where's himself? where's the master?" But by this time Mrs. Gunliffe was in an agony of despair, and was calling out for assistance lustily. Happily Gunliffe, the father, was at hand, and with him a man from the neighbouring village.

"Will you not send for the doctor?" said Mally. "Oh, man, you should send for the doctor!"

Whether any orders were given for the doctor she did not know, but in a very few minutes she was hurrying across the field again towards the path to the cove, and Gunliffe with the other man and his wife were following her.

As Mally went along she recovered her voice, for their step was not so quick as hers, and that which to them was a hurried movement, allowed her to get her breath again. And as she went she tried to explain to the father what had happened, saying but little, however, of her own doings in the matter. The wife hung behind listening, exclaiming every now and again that her boy was killed, and then asking wild questions as to his being yet alive. The father, as he went, said little. He was known as a silent, sober man, well spoken of for diligence and general conduct, but supposed to be stern and very hard when angered.

As they drew near to the top of the path, the other man whispered something to him, and then he turned round upon Mally and stopped her.

"If he has come by his death between you, your blood shall be taken for his," said he.

Then the wife shrieked out that her child had been murdered, and Mally, looking round into the faces of the three, saw that her grandfather's words had come true. They suspected her of having taken the life, in saving which she had nearly lost her own.

She looked round at them with awe in her face, and then, without saying a word, preceded them down the path. What had she to answer when such a charge as that was made against her? If they chose to say that she pushed him into the pool, and hit him with her hook as he lay amidst the waters, how could she show that it was not so?

Poor Mally knew little of the law of evidence, and it seemed to her that she was in their hands. But as she went down the steep track with a hurried step,—a step so quick that they could not keep up with her,—her heart was very full,—very full and very high. She had striven for the man's life as though he had been her brother. The blood was yet not dry on her own legs and arms, where she had torn them in his service. At one moment she had felt sure that she would die with him in that pool. And now they said that she had murdered him! It may be that he was not dead, and what would he say if ever he should speak again? Then she thought of that moment when his eyes had opened, and he had seemed to see her. She had no fear for herself, for her heart was very high. But it was full also,—full of scorn, disdain, and wrath.

When she had reached the bottom, she stood close to the door of the hut waiting for them, so that they might precede her to the other group, which was there in front of them, at a little distance on the sand.

"He is there, and dada is with him. Go and look at him," said Mally.

The father and mother ran on stumbling over the stones, but Mally remained behind by the door of the hut.

Barty Gunliffe was lying on the sand where Mally had left him, and old Malachi Trenglos was standing over him, resting himself with difficulty upon a stick.

"Not a move he's moved since she left him," said he, "not a move. I put his head on the old rug as you see, and I tried 'un with a drop of gin, but he wouldn't take it,—he wouldn't take it."

"Oh, my boy! my boy!" said the mother, throwing herself beside her son upon the sand.

"Haud your tongue, woman," said the father, kneeling down slowly by the lad's head, "whimpering that way will do 'un no good."

Then having gazed for a minute or two upon the pale face beneath him, he looked up sternly into that of Malachi Trenglos.

The old man hardly knew how to bear this terrible inquisition.

"He would come," said Malachi; "he brought it all upon hisself."

"Who was it struck him?" said the father.

"Sure he struck hisself, as he fell among the breakers."

"Liar!" said the father, looking up at the old man.

"They have murdered him!—they have murdered him!" shrieked the mother.

"Haud your peace, woman!" said the husband again. "They shall give us blood for blood."

Mally, leaning against the corner of the hovel, heard it all, but did not stir. They might say what they liked. They might make it out to be murder. They might drag her and her grandfather to Camelford Gaol, and then to Bodmin, and the gallows; but they could not take from her the conscious feeling that was her own. She had done her best to save him,—her very best. And she had saved him!

She remembered her threat to him before they had gone

down on the rocks together, and her evil wish. Those words had been very wicked; but since that she had risked her life to save his. They might say what they pleased of her, and do what they pleased. She knew what she knew.

Then the father raised his son's head and shoulders in his arms, and called on the others to assist him in carrying Barty towards the path. They raised him between them carefully and tenderly, and lifted their burden on towards the spot at which Mally was standing. She never moved, but watched them at their work; and the old man followed them, hobbling after them with his crutch.

When they had reached the end of the hut she looked upon Barty's face, and saw that it was very pale. There was no longer blood upon the forehead, but the great gash was to be seen there plainly, with its jagged cut, and the skin livid and blue round the orifice. His light brown hair was hanging back, as she had made it to hang when she had gathered it with her hand after the big wave had passed over them. Ah, how beautiful he was in Mally's eyes with that pale face, and the sad scar upon his brow! She turned her face away, that they might not see her tears; but she did not move, nor did she speak.

But now, when they had passed the end of the hut, shuffling along with their burden, she heard a sound which stirred her. She roused herself quickly from her leaning posture, and stretched forth her head as though to listen; then she moved to follow them. Yes, they had stopped at the bottom of the path, and had again laid the body on the rocks. She heard that sound again, as of a long, long sigh, and then, regardless of any of them, she ran to the wounded man's head.

"He is not dead," she said. "There; he is not dead."

As she spoke Barty's eyes opened, and he looked about him.

"Barty, my boy, speak to me," said the mother.

Barty turned his face upon his mother, smiled, and then stared about him wildly.

"How is it with thee, lad?" said his father. Then Barty turned his face again to the latter voice, and as he did so his eyes fell upon Mally.

"Mally!" he said, "Mally!"

It could have wanted nothing further to any of these present to teach them that, according to Barty's own view of the case, Mally had not been his enemy; and, in truth, Mally herself wanted no further triumph. That word had vindicated her, and she withdrew back to the hut.

"Dada," she said, "Barty is not dead, and I'm thinking they won't say anything more about our hurting him."

Old Glos shook his head. He was glad the lad hadn't met his death there; he didn't want the young man's blood, but he knew what folk would say. The poorer he was the more sure the world would be to trample on him. Mally said what she could to comfort him, being full of comfort herself.

She would have crept up to the farm if she dared, to ask how Barty was. But her courage failed her when she thought of that, so she went to work again, dragging back the weed she had saved to the spot at which on the morrow she would load the donkey. As she did this she saw Barty's pony still standing patiently under the rock, so she got a lock of fodder and threw it down before the beast.

It had become dark down in the cove, but she was still dragging back the sea-weed, when she saw the glimmer of a lantern coming down the pathway. It was a most unusual sight, for lanterns were not common down in Malachi's Cove. Down came the lantern rather slowly,—much more slowly than she was in the habit of descending, and then through the gloom she saw the figure of a man standing at the bottom of the path. She went up to him, and saw that it was Mr. Gunliffe, the father.

"Is that Mally?" said Gunliffe.

"Yes, it is Mally; and how is Barty, Mr. Gunliffe?"

"You must come to 'un yourself, now at once," said the farmer. "He won't sleep a wink till he's seed you. You must not say but you'll come."

"Sure I'll come if I'm wanted," said Mally.

Gunliffe waited a moment, thinking that Mally might have to prepare herself, but Mally needed no preparation. She was dripping with salt water from the weed which she had been dragging, and her elfin locks were streaming wildly from her head; but, such as she was, she was ready.

"Dada's in bed," she said, "and I can go now if you please."

Then Gunliffe turned round and followed her up the path, wondering at the life which this girl led so far away from all her sex. It was now dark night, and he had found her working at the very edge of the rolling waves by herself, in the darkness, while the only human being who might seem to be her protector had already gone to his bed.

When they were at the top of the cliff Gunliffe took her by her hand, and led her along. She did not comprehend this, but she made no attempt to take her hand from his. Something he said about falling on the cliffs, but it was muttered so lowly that Mally hardly understood him. But, in truth, the man knew that she had saved his boy's life, and that he had injured her instead of thanking her. He was now taking her to his heart, and as words were wanting to him, he was showing his love after this silent fashion. He held her by the hand as though she were a child, and Mally tripped along at his side asking him no questions.

When they were at the farm-yard gate, he stopped there for a moment.

"Mally, my girl," he said, "he'll not be content till he sees thee, but thou must not stay long wi' him, lass. Doctor says he's weak like, and wants sleep badly."

Mally merely nodded her head, and then they entered the house. Mally had never been within it before, and looked about with wondering eyes at the furniture of the big kitchen. Did any idea of her future destiny flash upon her then, I wonder? But she did not pause here a moment, but was led up to the bedroom above stairs, where Barty was lying on his mother's bed.

"Is it Mally herself?" said the voice of the weak youth.

"It's Mally herself," said the mother, "so now you can say what you please."

"Mally," said he, "Mally, it's along of you that I'm alive this moment."

"I'll not forget it on her," said the father, with his eyes turned away from her. "I'll never forget it on her."

"We hadn't a one but only him," said the mother, with her

apron up to her face.

"Mally, you'll be friends with me now?" said Barty.

To have been made lady of the manor of the cove for ever, Mally couldn't have spoken a word now. It was not only that the words and presence of the people there cowed her and made her speechless, but the big bed, and the looking-glass, and the unheard-of wonders of the chamber, made her feel her own insignificance. But she crept up to Barty's side, and put her hand upon his.

"I'll come and get the weed, Mally; but it shall all be for you," said Barty.

"Indeed, you won't then, Barty dear," said the mother; "you'll never go near the awesome place again. What would we do if you were took from us?"

"He mustn't go near the hole if he does," said Mally, speaking at last in a solemn voice, and imparting the knowledge which she had kept to herself while Barty was her enemy; " 'specially not if the wind's any way from the nor'ard."

"She'd better go down now," said the father.

Barty kissed the hand which he held, and Mally, looking at him as he did so, thought that he was like an angel.

"You'll come and see us to-morrow, Mally," said he.

To this she made no answer, but followed Mrs. Gunliffe out of the room. When they were down in the kitchen, the mother had tea for her, and thick milk, and a hot cake,—all the delicacies which the farm could afford. I don't know that Mally cared much for the eating and drinking that night, but she began to think that the Gunliffes were good people,—very good people. It was better thus, at any rate, than being accused of murder and carried off to Camelford prison.

"I'll never forget it on her—never," the father had said.

Those words stuck to her from that moment, and seemed to sound in her ears all the night. How glad she was that Barty had come down to the cove,—oh, yes, how glad! There was no question of his dying now, and as for the blow on his forehead, what harm was that to a lad like him?

"But father shall go with you," said Mrs. Gunliffe, when Mally prepared to start for the cove by herself. Mally, however, would not hear of this. She could find her way to the cove whether it was light or dark.

"Mally, thou art my child now, and I shall think of thee so," said the mother, as the girl went off by herself.

Mally thought of this, too, as she walked home. How could she become Mrs. Gunliffe's child; ah, how?

I need not, I think, tell the tale any further. That Mally did become Mrs. Gunliffe's child, and how she became so the reader will understand; and in process of time the big kitchen and all the wonders of the farm-house were her own. The people said that Barty Gunliffe had married a mermaid out of the sea; but when it was said in Mally's hearing I doubt whether she liked it; and when Barty himself would call her a mermaid she would frown at him, and throw about her black hair, and pretend to cuff him with her little hand.

Old Glos was brought up to the top of the cliff, and lived his few remaining days under the roof of Mr. Gunliffe's house; and as for the cove and the right of sea-weed, from that time forth all that has been supposed to attach itself to Gunliffe's farm, and I do not know that any of the neighbours are prepared to dispute the right.

Father Giles of Ballymoy

It is nearly thirty years since I, Archibald Green, first entered
the little town of Ballymoy, in the west of Ireland, and became
acquainted with one of the honestest fellows and best Christians whom it was ever been my good fortune to know. For
twenty years he and I were fast friends, though he was much
my elder. As he has now been ten years beneath the sod, I may
tell the story of our first meeting.[2]

Ballymoy is a so-called town—or was in the days of which I
am speaking—lying close to the shores of Lough Corrib, in the
country of Galway. It is on the road to no place, and, as the end
of a road, has in itself nothing to attract a traveller. The scenery
of Lough Corrib is grand; but the lake is very large, and the fine
scenery is on the side opposite to Ballymoy, and hardly to be
reached, or even seen, from that place. There is fishing—but it
is lake fishing. The salmon fishing of Lough Corrib is far away
from Ballymoy, where the little river runs away from the lake
down to the town of Galway. There was then in Ballymoy one
single street, of which the characteristic at first sight most
striking to a stranger was its general appearance of being
thoroughly wet through. It was not simply that the rain water
was generally running down its unguttered streets in muddy,
random rivulets, hurrying towards the lake with true Irish
impetuosity, but that each separate house looked as though the
walls were reeking with wet; and the alternated roofs of thatch
and slate—the slated houses being just double the height of
those that were thatched—assisted the eye and mind of the
spectator in forming this opinion. The lines were broken
everywhere, and at every break it seemed as though there was a
free entrance for the waters of heaven. The population of
Ballymoy was its second wonder. There had been no famine
then; no rot among the potatoes; and land round Ballymoy had
been let for nine, ten, and even eleven pounds an acre. At all
hours of the day, and at nearly all hours of the night, able-
bodied men were to be seen standing in the streets, with
knee-breeches unbuttoned, with stockings rolled down over

their brogues, and with swallow-tailed frieze coats. Nor, though thus idle, did they seem to suffer any of the distress of poverty. There were plenty of beggars, no doubt, in Ballymoy, but it never struck me that there was much distress in those days. The earth gave forth its potatoes freely, and neither man nor pig wanted more.

It was to be my destiny to stay a week at Ballymoy, on business, as to the nature of which I need not trouble the present reader. I was not, at that time, so well acquainted with the manners of the people of Connaught as I became afterwards, and I had certain misgivings as I was driven into the village on a jaunting-car from Tuam. I had just come down from Dublin, and had been informed there that there were two "hotels" in Ballymoy, but that one of the "hotels" might, perhaps, be found deficient on some of those comforts which I, as an Englishman, might require. I was therefore to ask for the "hotel" kept by Pat Kirwan. The other hotel was kept by Larry Kirwan; so that it behoved me to be particular. I had made the journey down from Dublin in a night and a day, travelling, as we then did travel in Ireland, by canal boats and by Bianconi's long cars; and I had dined at Tuam, and been driven over, after dinner on an April evening; and when I reached Ballymoy I was tired to death and very cold.[3]

"Pat Kirwan's hotel," I said to the driver, almost angrily. "Mind you don't go to the other."

"Shure, yer honour, and why not to Larry's? You'd be getting better enthertainment at Larry's, because of Father Giles."

I understood nothing about Father Giles, and wished to understand nothing. But I did understand that I was to go to Pat Kirwan's "hotel," and thither I insisted on being taken.

It was quite dusk at this time, and the wind was blowing down the street of Ballymoy, carrying before it wild gusts of rain. In the west of Ireland March weather comes in April, and it comes with a violence of its own, though not with the cruelty of the English east wind. At this moment my neck was ricked by my futile endeavours to keep my head straight on the side car, and the water had got under me upon the seat, and the horse had come to a stand-still half-a-dozen times in the last two minutes, and my apron had been trailed in the mud, and I was very unhappy. For the last ten minutes I had been thinking evil of everything Irish, and especially of Connaught.

I was driven up to a queerly-shaped, three-cornered house, that stood at the bottom of the street, and which seemed to possess none of the outside appurtenances of an inn.

"Is this Pat Kirwan's hotel?" said I.

"Faix, and it is then, yer honour," said the driver. "And barring only that Father Giles——"

But I had rung the bell, and as the door was now opened by a barefooted girl, I entered the little passage without hearing anything further about Father Giles.

"Could I have a bedroom immediately, with a fire in it?"

Not answering me directly, the girl led me into a sitting-room, in which my nose was at once greeted by that peculiar perfume which is given out by the relics of hot whisky-punch mixed with a great deal of sugar, and there she left me.

"Where is Pat Kirwan himself?" said I, coming to the door, and blustering somewhat. For, let it be remembered, I was very tired and it may be a fair question whether in the far west of Ireland a little bluster may not sometimes be of service. "If you have not a room ready, I will go to Larry Kirwan's," said I, showing that I understood the bearings of the place.

"It's right away at the furder end then, yer honour," said the driver, putting in his word, "and we comed by it ever so long since. But shure yer honour wouldn't think of leaving this house for that?"

This he said because Pat Kirwan's wife was close behind him.

Then Mrs. Kirwan assured me that I could and should be accommodated. The house, to be sure, was crowded, but she had already made arrangements, and had a bed ready. As for a fire in my bedroom, she could not recommend that, "becase the wind blew so mortial sthrong down the chimney since the pot had blown off—bad cess to it; and that loon, Mick Hackett, wouldn't lend a hand to put it up again, becase there were jobs going on at the big house—bad luck to every joint of his body, thin," said Mrs. Kirwan, with great energy. Nevertheless, she and Mick Hackett the mason were excellent friends.

I professed myself ready to go at once to the bedroom without the fire, and was led away up stairs. I asked where I was to eat my breakfast and dine on the next day, and was assured that I should have the room so strongly perfumed with whisky all to myself. I had been rather cross before, but on hearing this, I became decidedly sulky. It was not that I could not eat my breakfast in the chamber in question, but that I saw before me seven days of absolute misery, if I could have no other place of refuge for myself than a room in which, as was too plain, all Ballymoy came to drink and smoke. But there was no alternative, at any rate for that night and the following morning, and I therefore gulped down my anger without further spoken complaint, and followed the barefooted maiden upstairs, seeing my portmanteau carried up before me.

Ireland is not very well known now to all Englishmen, but it is much better known than it was in those days. On this my first visit into Connaught, I own that I was somewhat scared lest I should be made a victim of the wild lawlessness and general savagery of the people; and I fancied, as in the wet, windy gloom of the night, I could see the crowd of natives standing round the doors of the inn, and just discern their naked legs and old battered hats, that Ballymoy was probably one of those places so far removed from civilisation and law, as to be an unsafe residence for an English Protestant. I had undertaken the service on which I was employed, with my eyes more or less open, and was determined to go through with it—but I confess that I was by this time alive to its dangers. It was an early resolution with me, that I would not allow my portmanteau to be out of my sight. To that I would cling; with that ever close to me would I live; on that, if needful, would I die. I therefore required that it should be carried up the narrow stairs before me, and I saw it deposited safely in the bedroom.

The stairs were very narrow and very steep. Ascending them was like climbing into a loft. The whole house was built in a barbarous, uncivilised manner, and as fit to be an hotel as it was to be a church. It was triangular and all corners—the most uncomfortably arranged building I had ever seen. From the top of the stairs I was called upon to turn abruptly into the room destined for me; but there was a side step which I had not noticed under the glimmer of the small tallow candle, and I stumbled headlong into the chamber, uttering imprecations against Pat Kirwan, Ballymoy, and all Connaught.

I hope the reader will remember that I had travelled for thirty consecutive hours, had passed sixteen in a small comfortless canal boat without the power of stretching my legs, and that the wind had been at work upon me sideways for the last three hours. I was terribly tired, and I spoke very uncivilly to the young woman.

"Shure, yer honour, it's as clane as clane, and as dhry as dhry, and has been slept in every night since the big storm," said the girl, good-humouredly. Then she went on to tell me something more about Father Giles, of which, however I could catch nothing, as she was bending over the bed, folding down the bedclothes. "Feel of 'em," said she, "they's dhry as dhry."

I did feel them, and the sheets were dry and clean, and the bed, though very small, looked as if it would be comfortable. So I somewhat softened my tone to her, and bade her call me the next morning at eight.

"Shure, yer honour, and Father Giles will call yer hisself," said the girl.

I begged that Father Giles might be instructed to do no such thing. The girl, however, insisted that he would and then left me. Could it be that in this savage place, it was considered to be the duty of the parish priest to go round, with matins perhaps, or some other abominable papist ceremony, to the beds of all the strangers? My mother, who was a strict woman, had warned me vehemently against the machinations of the Irish priests, and I, in truth, had been disposed to ridicule her. Could it be that there were such machinations? Was it possible that my trousers might be refused me till I have taken mass? Or that force would be put upon me in some other shape, perhaps equally disagreeable?[4]

Regardless of that and other horrors, or rather, I should

perhaps say, determined to face manfully whatever horrors the night or morning might bring upon me, I began to prepare for bed. There was something pleasant in the romance of sleeping at Pat Kirwan's house in Ballymoy, instead of in my own room in Keppel Street, Russell Square.[5] So I chuckled inwardly at Pat Kirwan's idea of an hotel, and unpacked my things.

There was a little table covered with a clean cloth, on which I espied a small comb. I moved the comb carefully without touching it, and brought the table up to my bedside. I put out my brushes and clean linen for the morning, said my prayers, defying Father Giles and his machinations, and jumped into bed. The bed certainly was good, and the sheets were very pleasant. In five minutes I was fast asleep.

How long I had slept when I was awakened, I never knew. But it was at some hour in the dead of night, when I was disturbed by footsteps in my room, and on jumping up, I saw a tall, stout, elderly man standing with his back towards me, in the middle of the room, brushing his clothes with the utmost care. His coat was still on his back, and his pantaloons on his legs; but he was most assiduous in his attention to every part of his body which he could reach.

I sat upright, gazing at him, as I thought then, for ten minutes—we will say that I did so perhaps for forty seconds— and of one thing I became perfectly certain—namely, that the clothes-brush was my own! Whether, according to Irish hotel law, a gentleman would be justified in entering a stranger's room at midnight for the sake of brushing his clothes, I could not say; but I felt quite sure than in such a case, he would be bound at least to use the hotel brush or his own. There was a manifest trespass in regard to my property.

"Sir," said I, speaking very sharply, with the idea of startling him, "what are you doing here in this chamber?"

"Deed, then, and I'm sorry I've waked ye, my boy," said the stout gentleman.

"Will you have the goodness, sir, to tell me what you are doing here?"

"Bedad, then, just at this moment it's brushing my clothes, I am. It was badly they wanted it."

"I daresay they did. And you were doing it with my clothes-brush."

"And that's thrue too. And if a man hasn't a clothes-brush of his own, what else can he do but use somebody else's?"

"I think it's a great liberty, sir," said I.

"And I think it's a little one. It's only in the size of it we differ. But I beg your pardon. There is your brush. I hope it will be none the worse."

Then he put down the brush, seated himself on one of the two chairs which the room contained, and slowly proceeded to pull off his shoes, looking me full in the face all the while.

"What are you going to do, sir," said I, getting a little further out from under the clothes, and leaning over the table.

"I am going to bed," said the gentleman.

"Going to bed! where?"

"Here," said the gentleman; and he still went on untying the knot of his shoe-string.

It had always been a theory with me, in regard not only to my own country, but to all others, that civilisation displays itself never more clearly than when it ordains that every man shall have a bed for himself. In older days Englishmen of good position—men supposed to be gentlemen—would sleep together and think nothing of it, as ladies, I am told, will still do. And in outlandish regions, up to this time, the same practice prevails. In parts of Spain you will be told that one bed offers sufficient accommodation for two men, and in Spanish America the traveller is considered to be fastidious who thinks that one on each side of him is oppressive. Among the poorer classes with ourselves this grand touchstone of civilisation has not yet made itself felt. For aught I know there might be no such touchstone in Connaught at all. There clearly seemed to be none such at Ballymoy.

"You can't go to bed here," said I, sitting bolt upright on the couch.

"You'll find you are wrong there, my friend," said the elderly gentleman. "But make yourself aisy, I won't do you the least harm in life, and I sleep as quiet as a mouse."

It was quite clear to me that time had come for action. I

certainly would not let this gentleman get into my bed. I had been the first comer, and was for the night, at least, the proprietor of this room. Whatever might be the custom of this country in these wild regions, there could be no special law in the land justifying the landlord in such treatment of me as this.

"You won't sleep here, sir," said I, jumping out of the bed, over the table, on to the floor, and confronting the stranger just as he had succeeded in divesting himself of his second shoe. "You won't sleep here tonight, and so you may as well go away."

With that I picked up his two shoes, took them to the door, and chucked them out. I heard them go rattling down the stairs, and I was glad that they made so much noise. He would see that I was quite in earnest.

"You must follow your shoes," said I, "and the sooner the better."

I had not even yet seen the man very plainly, and even now, at this time, I hardly did so, though I went close up to him and put my hand upon his shoulder. The light was very imperfect, coming from one small farthing candle, which was nearly burnt out in the socket. And I, myself, was confused, ill at ease, and for the moment unobservant. I knew that the man was older than myself, but I had not recognised him as being old enough to demand or enjoy personal protection by reason of his age. He was tall, and big, and burly—as he appeared to me then. Hitherto, till his shoes had been chucked away, he had maintained impertubable good-humour. When he heard the shoes clattering down-stairs, it seemed that he did not like it, and he began to talk fast and in an angry voice. I would not argue with him, and I did not understand him, but still keeping my hand on the collar of his coat, I insisted that he should not sleep there. Go away out of that chamber he should.

"But it's my own," he said, shouting the words a dozen times. "It's my own room. It's my own room."

So this was Pat Kirwan himself—drunk probably, or mad.

"It may be your own," said I; "but you've let it to me for tonight, and you shan't sleep here;" so saying I backed him towards the door, and in so doing I trod upon his unguarded toe.

"Bother you, thin, for a pig-headed Englishman!" said he. "You've kilt me entirely now. So take your hands off my neck, will ye, before you have me throttled outright!"

I was sorry to have trod on his toe, but I stuck to him all the same. I had him near the door now, and I was determined to put him out into the passage. His face was very round and very red, and I thought that he must be drunk; and since I had found out that it was Pat Kirwan the landlord, I was more angry with the man than ever.

"You shan't sleep here, so you might as well go," I said, as I backed him away towards the door. This had not been closed since the shoes had been thrown out, and with something of a struggle between the doorposts, I got him out. I remembered nothing whatever as to the suddenness of the stairs. I had been fast asleep since I came up them, and hardly even as yet knew exactly where I was. So, when I got him through the aperture of the door, I gave him a push, as was most natural, I think, for me to do. Down he went backwards—down the stairs, all in a heap, and I could hear that in his fall he had stumbled against Mrs. Kirwan, who was coming up, doubtless to ascertain the cause of all the trouble above her head.

A hope crossed my mind that the wife might be of assistance to her husband in this time of his trouble. The man had fallen very heavily, I knew, and had fallen backwards. And I remembered then how steep the stairs were. Heaven and earth! Suppose that he were killed—or even seriously injured in his own house. What, in such case as that, would my life be worth in that wild country? Then I began to regret that I had been so hot. It might be that I had murdered a man on my first entrance into Connaught!

For a moment or two I could not make up my mind what I would first do. I was aware that both the landlady and the servant were occupied with the body of the ejected occupier of my chamber, and I was aware also that I had nothing on but my night-shirt. I returned, therefore, within the door, but could not bring myself to shut myself in and return to bed without making some inquiry as to the man's fate. I put my head out, therefore, and did make inquiry.

"I hope he is not much hurt by his fall," I said.

"Ochone, ochone! murdher, murdher! Spake, Father Giles, dear, for the love of God!" Such and many such exclamations I heard from the women at the bottom of the stairs.

"I hope he is not much hurt," I said again, putting my head out from the doorway: "But he shouldn't have forced himself into my room."

"His room, the omadhaun!—the born idiot!" said the land-lady.

"Faix, ma'am, and Father Giles is a dead man," said the girl, who was kneeling over the prostrate body in the passage below.

I heard her say Father Giles as plain as possible, and then I became aware that the man whom I had thrust out was not the landlord, but the priest of the parish! My heart became sick within me as I thought of the troubles around me. And I was sick also with fear lest the man who had fallen should be seriously hurt. But why—why—why had he forced his way into my room? How was it to be expected that I should have remembered that the stairs of the accursed house came flush up to the door of the chamber?

"He shall be hanged if there's law in Ireland," said a voice down below; and as far as I could see it might be that I should be hung. When I heard that last voice I began to think that I had in truth killed a man, and a cold sweat broke out all over me, and I stood for awhile shivering where I was. Then I remembered that it behoved me as a man to go down among my enemies below, and to see what had really happened, to learn whom I had hurt—let the consequences to myself be what they might. So I quickly put on some of my clothes,—a pair of trousers, a loose coat, and a pair of slippers, and I descended the stairs. By this time they had taken the priest into the whisky-perfumed chamber below, and although the hour was late there were already six or seven persons with him. Among them was the real Pat Kirwan himself, who had not been so particular about his costume as I had.

Father Giles—for indeed it was Father Giles, the priest of the parish—had been placed in an old arm-chair, and his head was resting against Mrs. Kirwan's body. I could tell from the moans which he emitted that there was still, at any rate, hope of life.

Pat Kirwan, who did not quite understand what had happened, and who was still half asleep, and as I afterwards learned, half tipsy, was standing over him wagging his head. The girl was also standing by, with an old woman and two men who had made their way in through the kitchen.

"Have you sent for a doctor?" said I.

"Oh, you born blagghuard!" said the woman. "You thief of the world! That the like of you should ever have darkened my door!"

"You can't repent it more than I do, Mrs. Kirwan; but hadn't you better send for the doctor?"

"Faix, and for the police too, you may be shure of that, young man. To go and chuck him out of the room like that— his own room, too, and he a priest and an ould man—he that had given up the half of it, though I axed him not to do so, for a sthranger as nobody knowed nothing about."

The truth was coming out by degrees. Not only was the man I had put out Father Giles, but he was also the proper occupier of the room. At any rate somebody ought to have told me all this before they put me to sleep in the same bed with the priest.

I made my way round to the injured man, and put my hand upon his shoulder, thinking that perhaps I might be able to ascertain the extent of the injury. But the angry woman, together with the girl, drove me away, heaping on me terms of reproach, and threatening me with the gallows at Galway.

I was very anxious that a doctor should be brought as soon as possible; and as it seemed that nothing was being done, I offered to go and search for one. But I was given to understand that I should not be allowed to leave the house until the police had come. I had therefore to remain there for half-an-hour, or nearly so, till a sergeant, with two other policemen, really did come. During this time I was in a most wretched frame of mind. I knew no one at Ballymoy or in the neighbourhood. From the manner in which I was addressed, and also threatened by Mrs. Kirwan and by those who came in and out of the room, I was aware that I should encounter the most intense hostility. I had heard of Irish murders, and heard also of the love of the people for their priests, and I really began to doubt whether my life might not be in danger.

During this time, while I was thus waiting, Father Giles himself recovered his consciousness. He had been stunned by the fall, but his mind came back to him, though by no means all at once; and while I was left in the room with him he hardly seemed to remember all the events of the past hour.

I was able to discover from what was said that he had been for some days past, or, as it afterwards turned out for the last month, the tenant of the room, and that when I arrived he had been drinking tea with Mrs. Kirwan. The only other public bedroom in the hotel was occupied, and he had with great kindness given the landlady permission to put the Saxon stranger into his chamber. All this came out by degrees, and I could see how the idea of my base and cruel ingratitude rankled in the heart of Mrs. Kirwan. It was in vain that I expostulated and explained, and submitted myself humbly to everything that was said around me.

"But, ma'am," I said, "if I had only been told that it was the reverend gentleman's bed!"

"Bed, indeed! To hear the blagghuard talk you'd think it was axing Father Giles to sleep along with the likes of him we were. And there's two beds in the room as dacent as any Christian iver stretched in."

It was a new light to me. And yet I had known over night, before I undressed, that there were two bedsteads in the room! I had seen them, and had quite forgotten the fact in my confusion when I was woken. I had been very stupid, certainly. I felt that now. But I had truly believed that that big man was going to get into my little bed. It was terrible as I thought of it now. The good-natured priest, for the sake of accommodating a stranger, had consented to give up half of his room, and had been repaid for his kindness by being—perhaps murdered! And yet, though just then I hated myself cordially, I could not quite bring myself to look at the matter as they looked at it.

There were excuses to be made, if only I could get any one to listen to them.

"He was using my brush—my clothes-brush—indeed he was," I said. "Not but what he'd be welcome; but it made me think he was an intruder."

"And wasn't it too much honour for the likes of ye?" said one of the women, with infinite scorn in the tone of her voice.

"I did use the gentleman's clothes-brush, certainly," said the priest. They were the first collected words he had spoken, and I felt very grateful to him for them. It seemed to me that a man who could condescend to remember that he had used a clothes-brush, could not really be hurt to death, even though he had been pushed down such very steep stairs as those belonging to Pat Kirwan's hotel.

"And I'm sure you were very welcome, sir," said I. "It wasn't that I minded the clothes-brush. It wasn't, indeed; only I thought—indeed, I did think that there was only one bed. And they had put me into the room, and had not said anything about anybody else. And what was I to think when I woke up in the middle of the night?"

"Faix, and you'll have enough to think of in Galway gaol, for that's where you're going to," said one of the bystanders.

I can hardly explain the bitterness that was displayed against me. No violence was absolutely shown to me, but I could not move without eliciting a manifest determination that I was not to be allowed to stir out of the room. Red, angry eyes were glowering at me, and every word I spoke called down some expression of scorn and ill-will. I was beginning to feel glad that the police were coming, thinking that I needed protection. I was thoroughly ashamed of what I had done, and yet I could not discover that I had been very wrong at any particular moment. Let any man ask himself the question, what he would do, if he supposed that a stout old gentleman had entered his room at an inn and insisted on getting into his bed? It was not my fault that there had been no proper landing-place at the top of the stairs.

Two sub-constables had been in the room for some time before the sergeant came, and with the sergeant arrived also the doctor, and another priest—Father Columb he was called—who, as I afterwards learned, was curate or coadjutor to Father Giles. By this time there was quite a crowd in the house, although it was past one o'clock, and it seemed that all Ballymoy knew that its priest had been foully misused. It was manifest to me that there was something in the Roman Catholic religion which made the priests very dear to the people; for I doubt whether in any village in England, had such an accident happened to the rector, all the people would have roused themselves at midnight to wreak their vengeance on the assailant. For vengeance they were now beginning to clamour, and even before the sergeant of police had come, the two subconstables were standing over me; and I felt that they were protecting me from the people in order that they might give me up—to the gallows!

I did not like the Ballymoy doctor at all—then, or even at a later period of my visit to that town. On his arrival he made his way up to the priest through the crowd, and would not satisfy their affection or my anxiety by declaring at once that there was no danger. Instead of doing so he insisted on the terrible nature of the outrage and the brutality shown by the assailant. And at every hard word he said, Mrs. Kirwan would urge him on.

"That's thrue for you, doctor!" " 'Deed, and you may say that, doctor; two as good beds as ever Christian stretched in!" " 'Deed, and it was just Father Giles's own room, as you may say, since the big storm fetched the roof off his riverence's house below there."

Thus gradually I was learning the whole history. The roof had been blown off Father Giles's own house, and therefore he had gone to lodge at the inn! He had been willing to share his lodging with a stranger, and this had been his reward!

"I hope, doctor, that the gentleman is not much hurt," said I, very meekly.

"Do you suppose a gentleman like that, sir, can be thrown down a long flight of stairs without being hurt?" said the doctor, in an angry voice. "It is no thanks to you, sir, that his neck has not been sacrificed."

Then there arose a hum of indignation, and the two policemen standing over me bustled about a little, coming very close to me, as though they thought they should have something to do to protect me from being torn to pieces.

I bethought me that it was my special duty in such a crisis to show a spirit, if it were only for the honour of my Saxon blood among the Celts. So I spoke up again, as loud as I could well speak.

"No one in this room is more distressed at what has occurred than I am. I am most anxious to know, for the gentleman's sake, whether he has been seriously hurt?"

"Very seriously hurt indeed," said the doctor; "very seriously hurt. The vertebræ may have been injured for aught I know at present."

"Arrah, blazes, man," said a voice, which I learned afterwards had belonged to an officer of the revenue corps of men which was then stationed at Ballymoy, a gentleman with whom I became afterwards familiarly acquainted; Tom Macdermot was his name, Captain Tom Macdermot, and he came from the county of Leitrim—"Arrah, blazes, man; do ye think a gentleman's to fall sthrait headlong backwards down such a ladder as that, and not find it inconvanient? Only that he's the priest, and has had his own luck, sorrow a neck belonging to him there would be this minute."

"Be aisy, Tom," said Father Giles himself; and I was delighted to hear him speak. Then there was a pause for a moment. "Tell the gentleman I ain't so bad at all," said the priest; and from that moment I felt an affection to him which never afterwards waned.

They got him upstairs back into the room from which he had been evicted, and I was carried off to the police-station, where I positively spent the night. What a night it was! I had came direct from London, sleeping on my road but once in Dublin, and now I found myself accommodated with a stretcher in the police barracks at Ballymoy! And the worst of it was that I had business to do at Ballymoy which required that I should hold up my head and make much of myself. The few words which had been spoken by the priest had comforted me, and had enabled me to think again of my own position. Why was I locked up? No magistrate had committed me. It was really a question whether I had done anything illegal. As that man whom Father Giles called Tom had very properly explained, if people will have ladders instead of staircases in their houses, how is anybody to put an intruder out of the room without risk of breaking the intruder's neck? And as to the fact—now an undoubted fact—that Father Giles was no intruder, the fault in that lay with the Kirwans, who had told me nothing of the truth. The boards of the stretcher in the police-station were very hard, in spite of the blankets with which I had been furnished; and as I lay there I began to remind myself that there certainly must be law in county Galway. So I called to the attendant policeman and asked him by whose authority I was locked up.

"Ah, thin, don't bother," said the policeman; "shure, and you've given throuble enough this night!" The dawn was at that moment breaking so I turned myself on the stretcher, and resolved that I would put a bold face on it all when the day should come.

The first person I saw in the morning was Captain Tom, who came into the room where I was lying, followed by a little boy with my portmanteau. The sub-inspector of police who rules over the men at Ballymoy lived, as I afterwards learned, at Oranmore, so that I had not, at this conjuncture, the honour of seeing him. Captain Tom assured me that he was an excellent fellow, and rode to hounds like a bird. As in those days I rode to hounds myself—as nearly like a bird as I was able—I was glad to have such an account of my head-gaoler.[6] The sub-constables seemed to do just what Captain Tom told them, and there was, no doubt, a very good understanding between the police force and the revenue officer.

"Well, now, I'll tell you what you must do, Mr. Green," said the Captain.

"In the first place," said I, "I must protest that I'm now locked up here illegally."

"Oh, bother; now don't make yourself unaisy."

"That's all very well, Captain——. I beg your pardon, sir, but I didn't catch any name plainly except the Christian name."

"My name is Macdermot—Tom Macdermot. They call me Captain—but that's neither here nor there."

"I suppose, Captain Macdermot, the police here cannot lock up anybody they please, without a warrant?"

"And where would you have been if they hadn't locked you up? I'm blessed if they wouldn't have had you into the Lough before this time."

There might be something in that, and I therefore resolved to forgive the personal indignity which I had suffered, if I could secure something like just treatment for the future. Captain Tom had already told me that Father Giles was doing pretty well.

"He's as sthrong as a horse, you see, or, sorrow a doubt, he'd be a dead man this minute. The back of his neck is as black as your hat with the bruises, and its the same way with him all down his loins. A man like that, you know, not just as young as he was once, falls mortial heavy. But he's as jolly as a four-year old," said Captain Tom, "and you're to go and ate your breakfast with him, in his bedroom, so that you may see with your own eyes that there are two beds there."

"I remembered it afterwards quite well," said I.

" 'Deed, and Father Giles got such a kick of laughter this morning, when he came to understand that you thought he was going to get into bed alongside of you, and he strained himself all over again, and I thought he'd have frightened the house, yelling with the pain. But anyway you've to go over and see him. So now you'd better get yourself dressed."

This announcement was certainly very pleasant. Against Father Giles, of course, I had no feeling of bitterness. He had behaved well throughout, and I was quite alive to the fact that the light of his countenance would afford me a better ægis against the ill-will of the people of Ballymoy, than anything the law would do for me. So I dressed myself in the barrack-room, while Captain Tom waited without; and then I sallied out under his guidance to make a second visit to Pat Kirwan's hotel. I was amused to see that the police, though by no means subject to Captain Tom's orders, let me go without the least difficulty, and that the boy was allowed to carry my portmanteau away with him.

"Oh, it's all right," said Captain Tom when I alluded to this. "You're not down in the sheet. You were only there for protection, you know."

Nevertheless, I had been taken there by force, and had been locked up by force. If, however, they were disposed to forget all that, so was I. I did not return to the barracks again; and when, after that, the policeman whom I had known met me in the street, they always accosted me as though I were an old friend; hoping my honour had found a better bed than when they last saw me. They had not looked at me with any friendship in their eyes when they had stood over me in Pat Kirwan's parlour.

This was my first view of Ballymoy, and of the "hotel" by daylight. I now saw that Mrs. Pat Kirwan kept a grocery establishment, and that the three-cornered house which had so astonished me was very small. Had I seen it before I entered it, I should hardly have dared to look there for a night's lodging. As it was, I stayed there for a fortnight, and was by no means uncomfortable. Knots of men and women were now standing in groups round the door, and, indeed, the lower end of the street was almost crowded.

"They're all here," whispered Captain Tom, "because they've heard how Father Giles has been murdered during the night by a terrible Saxon; and there isn't a man or woman among them who doesn't know that you are the man who did it."

"But they know also, I suppose," said I, "that Father Giles is alive."

"Bedad, yes, they know that, or I wouldn't be in your skin, my boy. But come along. We mustn't keep the priest waiting for his breakfast."

I could see that they all looked at me, and there were some of them, especially among the women, whose looks I did not even yet like. They spoke among each other in Gaelic, and I could perceive that they were talking of me.

"Can't you understand, then," said Captain Tom, speaking to them aloud, just as he entered the house, "that Father Giles,

the Lord be praised, is as well as ever he was in his life? Shure it
was only an accident."

"An accident done on purpose, Captain Tom," said one
person.

"What is it to you how it was done, Mick Healy? If Father
Giles is satisfied, isn't that enough for the likes of you? Get
out of that, and let the gentleman pass." Then Captain Tom
pushed Mick away roughly, and the others let us enter the
house. "Only they wouldn't do it unless somebody gave them
the wink, they'd pull you in pieces this moment for a dandy of
punch—they would, indeed."

Perhaps Captain Tom exaggerated the prevailing feeling,
thinking thereby to raise the value of his own service in protecting me; but I was quite alive to the fact that I had done a
most dangerous deed, and had a most narrow escape.

I found Father Giles sitting up in his bed, while Mrs. Kirwan
was rubbing his shoulder diligently with an embrocation of
arnica. The girl was standing by with a basin half full of the
same, and I could see that the priest's neck and shoulders were
as red as a raw beefsteak. He winced grievously under the
rubbing, but he bore it like a man.

"And here comes the hero," said Father Giles. "Now stop a
minute or two, Mrs. Kirwan, while we have a mouthful of
breakfast, for I'll go bail that Mr. Green is hungry after his
night's rest. I hope you got a better bed, Mr. Green, than the
one I found you in when I was unfortunate enough to waken
you last night. There it is, all ready for you still," said he; "and
if you accept of it tonight, take my advice and don't let a trifle
stand in the way of your dhraims."

"I hope, thin, the gintleman will contrive to suit hisself
elsewhere," said Mrs. Kirwan.

"He'll be very welcome to take up his quarters here if he
likes," said the priest. "And why not? But, bedad, sir, you'd
better be a little more careful the next time you see a stranger
using your clothes-brush. They are not so strict here in their
ideas of meum and tuum as they are perhaps in England; and if
you had broken my neck for so small an offence, I don't know
but what they'd have stretched your own."

We then had breakfast together, Father Giles, Captain Tom, and I; and a very good breakfast we had. By degrees even Mrs. Kirwan was induced to look favourably at me, and before the day was over I found myself to be regarded as a friend in the establishment. And as a friend I certainly was regarded by Father Giles—then, and for many a long day afterwards. And many times when he has, in years since that, but years nevertheless which are now long back, come over and visited me in my English home, he has told the story of the manner in which we first became acquainted.[7] "When you find a gentleman asleep," he would say, "always ask his leave before you take a liberty with his clothes-brush."

La Mère Bauche

The Pyreneean valley in which the baths of Vernet are situated is not much known to English, or indeed to any travellers. Tourists in search of good hotels and picturesque beauty combined, do not generally extend their journeys to the Eastern Pyrenees. They rarely get beyond Luchon; and in this they are right, as they thus end their peregrinations at the most lovely spot among these mountains; and are as a rule so deceived, imposed on, and bewildered by guides, innkeepers, and horse-owners at this otherwise delightful place as to become un-desirous of further travel. Nor do invalids from distant parts frequent Vernet. People of fashion go to the Eaux Bonnes and to Luchon, and people who are really ill to Baréges and Cauterets. It is at these places that one meets crowds of Parisians, and the daughters and wives of rich merchants from Bordeaux, with an admixture, now by no means inconsider-able, of Englishmen and Englishwomen. But the Eastern Pyrenees are still unfrequented. And probably they will re-main so; for though there are among them lovely valleys—and of all such the valley of Vernet is perhaps the most lovely—they cannot compete with the mountain scenery of other tourists-loved regions in Europe. At the Port de Venasquez and the Brèche de Roland in the Western Pyrenees, or rather, to speak more truly, at spots in the close vicinity of these famous mountain entrances from France into Spain, one can make comparisons with Switzerland, Northern Italy, the Tyrol, and Ireland, which will not be injurious to the scenes then under view. But among the eastern mountains this can rarely be done. The hills do not stand thickly together so as to group them-selves; the passes from one valley to another, though not wanting in altitude, are not close pressed together with over-hanging rocks, and are deficient in grandeur as well as loveli-ness. And then, as a natural consequence of all this, the hotels—are not quite as good as they should be.

But there is one mountain among them which can claim to rank with the Pic du Midi or the Maledetta. No one can pooh-pooh the stern old Canigou, standing high and solitary, solemn and grand, between the two roads which run from Perpignan into Spain, the one by Prades and the other by Le Boulon. Under the Canigou, towards the west, lie the hot baths of Vernet, in a close secluded valley, which, as I have said before is, as far as I know, the sweetest spot in these Eastern Pyrenees.

The frequenters of these baths were a few years back gathered almost entirely from towns not very far distant, from Perpignan, Narbonne, Carcassonne, and Bézières, and were not therefore famous, expensive, or luxurious; but those who believed in them believed with great faith; and it was certainly the fact that men and women who went thither worn with toil, sick with excesses, and nervous through over-care, came back fresh and strong, fit once more to attack the world with all its woes. Their character in latter days does not seem to have changed, though their circle of admirers may perhaps be somewhat extended.

In those days, by far the most noted and illustrious person in the village of Vernet was La Mère Bauche. That there had once been a Père Bauche was known to the world, for there was a Fils Bauche who lived with his mother; but no one seemed to remember more of him than that he had once existed. At Vernet he had never been known. La Mère Bauche was a native of the village, but her married life had been passed away from it, and she had returned in her early widowhood to become proprietress and manager, or, as one may say, the heart and soul of the Hôtel Bauche at Vernet.

This hotel was a large and somewhat rough establishment, intended for the accommodation of invalids who came to Vernet for their health. It was built immediately over one of the thermal springs, so that the water flowed from the bowels of the earth directly into the baths. There was accommodation for seventy people, and during the summer and autumn months the place was always full. Not a few also were to be found there during the winter and spring, for the charges of Madame Bauche were low, and the accommodation reasonably good.

And in this respect, as indeed in all others, Madame Bauche

had the reputation of being an honest woman. She had a certain price, from which no earthly consideration would induce her to depart; and certain returns for this price in the shape of déjeuners and dinners, baths and beds, which she never failed to give in accordance with the dictates of a strict conscience. These were traits in the character of an hotel-keeper which cannot be praised too highly, and which had met their due reward in the custom of the public. But nevertheless there were those who thought that there was occasionally ground for complaint in the conduct even of Madame Bauche.

In the first place she was deficient in that pleasant smiling softness which should belong to any keeper of a house of public entertainment. In her general mode of life she was stern and silent with her guests, autocratic, authoritative, and sometimes contradictory in her house, and altogether irrational and unconciliatory when any change even for a day was proposed to her, or when any shadow of a complaint reached her ears.

Indeed of complaint, as made against the establishment, she was altogether intolerant. To such she had but one answer. He or she who complained might leave the place at a moment's notice if it so pleased them. There were always others ready to take their places. The power of making this answer came to her from the lowness of her prices; and it was a power which was very dear to her.

The baths were taken at different hours according to medical advice, but the usual time was from five to seven in the morning. The déjeuner or early meal was at nine o'clock, the dinner was at four. After that, no eating or drinking was allowed in the Hôtel Bauche. There was a café in the village, at which ladies and gentlemen could get a cup of coffee or a glass of *eau sucré*; but no such accommodation was to be had in the establishment. Not by any possible bribery or persuasion could any meal be procured at any other than the authorized hours. A visitor who should enter the *salle à manger* more than ten minutes after the last bell would be looked at very sourly by Madame Bauche, who on all occasions sat at the top of her own table. Should any one appear as much as half an hour late, he would receive only his share of what had not been handed round. But after the last dish had been so handed, it was utterly useless for any one to enter the room at all.

Her appearance at the period of our tale was perhaps not altogether in her favour. She was about sixty years of age and was very stout and short in the neck. She wore her own grey hair, which at dinner was always tidy enough; but during the whole day previous to that hour she might be seen with it escaping from under her cap in extreme disorder. Her eyebrows were large and bushy, but those alone would not have given to her face that look of indomitable sternness which it possessed. Her eyebrows were serious in their effect, but not so serious as the pair of green spectacles which she always wore under them. It was thought by those who had analyzed the subject that the great secret of Madame Bauche's power lay in her green spectacles.

Her custom was to move about and through the whole establishment every day from breakfast till the period came for her to dress for dinner. She would visit every chamber and every bath, walk once or twice round the *salle à manger*, and very repeatedly round the kitchen; she would go into every hole and corner, and peer into everything through her green spectacles: and in these walks it was not always thought pleasant to meet her. Her custom was to move very slowly, with her hands generally clasped behind her back: she rarely spoke to the guests unless she was spoken to, and on such occasions she would not often diverge into general conversation. If any one had aught to say connected with the business of the establishment, she would listen, and then she would make her answers,—often not pleasant in the hearing.

And thus she walked her path through the world, a stern, hard solemn old woman, not without gusts of passionate explosion; but honest withal, and not without some inward benevolence and true tenderness of heart. Children she had had many, some seven or eight. One or two had died, others had been married; she had sons settled far away from home, and at the time of which we are now speaking but one was left in any way subject to parental authority.

Adolphe Bauche was the only one of her children of whom

much was remembered by the present denizens and hangers-on of the hotel. He was the youngest of the number, and having been born only very shortly before the return of Madame Bauche to Vernet, had been altogether reared there. It was thought by the world of those parts, and rightly thought, that he was his mother's darling—more so than had been any of his brothers and sisters,—the very apple of her eye, and gem of her life. At this time he was about twenty-five years of age, and for the last two years had been absent from Vernet—for reasons which will shortly be made to appear. He had been sent to Paris to see something of the world, and learn to talk French instead of the patois of his valley; and having left Paris had come down south into Languedoc, and remained there picking up some agricultural lore which it was thought might prove useful in the valley farms of Vernet. He was now expected home again very speedily, much to his mother's delight.

That she was kind and gracious to her favourite child does not perhaps give much proof of her benevolence; but she had also been kind and gracious to the orphan child of a neighbour; nay, to the orphan child of a rival innkeeper. At Vernet there had been more than one water establishment, but the proprietor of the second had died some few years after Madame Bauche had settled herself at the place. His house had not thrived, and his only child, a little girl, was left altogether without provision.

This little girl, Marie Clavert, La Mère Bauche had taken into her own house immediately after the father's death, although she had most cordially hated that father. Marie was then an infant, and Madame Bauche had accepted the charge without much thought, perhaps, as to what might be the child's ultimate destiny. But since then she had thoroughly done the duty of a mother by the little girl, who had become the pet of the whole establishment, the favourite plaything of Adolphe Bauche,—and at last of course his early sweetheart.

And then and therefore there had come troubles at Vernet. Of course all the world of the valley had seen what was taking place and what was likely to take place, long before Madame Bauche knew anything about it. But at last it broke upon her senses that her son, Adolphe Bauche, the heir to all her virtues and all her riches, the first young man in that or any neighbouring valley, was absolutely contemplating the idea of marrying that poor little orphan, Marie Clavert!

That any one should ever fall in love with Marie Clavert had never occured to Madame Bauche. She had always regarded the child as a child, as the object of her charity, and as a little thing to be looked on as poor Marie by all the world. She, looking through her green spectacles, had never seen that Marie Clavert was a beautiful creature, full of ripening charms, such as young men love to look on. Marie was of infinite daily use to Madame Bauche in a hundred little things about the house, and the old lady thoroughly recognized and appreciated her ability. But for this very reason she had never taught herself to regard Marie otherwise than as a useful drudge. She was very fond of her protégé—so much so that she would listen to her in affairs about the house when she would listen to no one else;—but Marie's prettiness and grace and sweetness as a girl had all been thrown away upon Maman Bauche, as Marie used to call her.

But unluckily it had not been thrown away upon Adolphe. He had appreciated, as it was natural that he should do, all that had been so utterly indifferent to his mother; and consequently had fallen in love. Consequently also he had told his love; and consequently also, Marie had returned his love. Adolphe had been hitherto contradicted but in few things, and thought that all difficulty would be prevented by his informing his mother that he wished to marry Marie Clavert. But Marie, with a woman's instinct, had known better. She had trembled and almost crouched with fear when she confessed her love; and had absolutely hid herself from sight when Adolphe went forth, prepared to ask his mother's consent to his marriage.

The indignation and passionate wrath of Madame Bauche were past and gone two years before the date of this story, and I need not therefore much enlarge upon that subject. She was at first abusive and bitter, which was bad for Marie; and afterwards bitter and silent, which was worse. It was of course determined that poor Marie should be sent away to some asylum for orphans or penniless paupers—in short anywhere out of the way. What mattered her outlook into the world, her happiness, or indeed her very existence? The outlook and happiness of Adolphe Bauche,—was not that to be considered as everything at Vernet?

But this terrible sharp aspect of affairs did not last very long. In the first place La Mère Bauche had under those green spectacles a heart that in truth was tender and affectionate, and after the first two days of anger she admitted that something must be done for Marie Clavert; and after the fourth day she acknowledged that the world of the hotel, her world, would not go as well without Marie Clavert as it would with her. And in the next place Madame Bauche had a friend whose advice in grave matters she would sometimes take. This friend had told her that it would be much better to send away Adolphe, since it was so necessary that there should be a sending away of some one; that he would be much benefited by passing some months of his life away from his native valley; and that an absence of a year or two would teach him to forget Marie, even if it did not teach Marie to forget him.

And we must say a word or two about this friend. At Vernet he was usually called M. le Capitaine, though in fact he had never reached that rank. He had been in the army, and having been wounded in the leg while still a sous-lieutenant, had been pensioned, and had thus been interdicted from treading any further the thorny path that leads to glory. For the last fifteen years he had resided under the roof of Madame Bauche, at first as a casual visitor, going and coming, but now for many years as constant there as she was herself.

He was so constantly called Le Capitaine that his real name was seldom heard. It may however as well be known to us that this was Theodore Campan. He was a tall, well-looking man; always dressed in black garments, of a coarse description certainly, but scrupulously clean and well brushed; of perhaps fifty years of age, and conspicuous for the rigid uprightness of his back—and for a black wooden leg.[8]

This wooden leg was perhaps the most remarkable trait in his character. It was always jet black, being painted, or polished, or japanned, as occasion might require, by the hands of the capitaine himself. It was longer than ordinary wooden legs, as indeed the capitaine was longer than ordinary men; but nevertheless it never seemed in any way to impede the rigid punctilious propriety of his movements. It was never in his way as wooden legs usually are in the way of their wearers. And then to render it more illustrious it had round its middle, round the calf of the leg we may so say, a band of bright brass which shone like burnished gold.

It had been the capitaine's custom, now for some years past, to retire every evening at about seven o'clock into the sanctum sanctorum of Madame Bauche's habitation, the dark little private sitting-room in which she made out her bills and calculated her profits, and there regale himself in her presence—and indeed at her expense,—for the items never appeared in the bill, with coffee, and cognac. I have said that there was neither eating nor drinking at the establishment after the regular dinner-hours; but in so saying I spoke of the world at large. Nothing further was allowed in the way of trade; but in the way of friendship so much was now-a-days always allowed to the capitaine.

It was at these moments that Madame Bauche discussed her private affairs, and asked for and received advice. For even Madame Bauche was mortal; nor could her green spectacles without other aid carry her through all the troubles of life. It was now five years since the world of Vernet discovered that La Mère Bauche was going to marry the capitaine; and for eighteen months the world of Vernet had been full of this matter: but any amount of patience is at last exhausted, and as no further steps in that direction were ever taken beyond the daily cup of coffee, that subject died away—very much unheeded by La Mère Bauche.

But she, though she thought of no matrimony for herself, thought much of matrimony for other people; and over most of those cups of evening coffee and cognac a matrimonial project was discussed in these latter days. It has been seen that the capitaine pleaded in Marie's favour when the fury of Madame Bauche's indignation broke forth; and that ultimately Marie was kept at home, and Adolphe sent away by his advice.

"But Adolphe cannot always stay away," Madame Bauche had pleaded in her difficulty. The truth of this the capitaine had admitted; but Marie, he said, might be married to some one else before two years were over. And so the matter had commenced.

But to whom should she be married? To this question the capitaine had answered in perfect innocence of heart, that La Mère Bauche would be much better able to make such a choice than himself. He did not know how Marie might stand with regard to money. If madame would give some little "dot," the affair, the capitaine thought, would be more easily arranged.

All these things took months to say, during which period Marie went on with her work in melancholy listlessness. One comfort she had. Adolphe, before he went, had promised to her, holding in his hand as he did so a little cross which she had given him, that no earthly consideration should sever them;— that sooner or later he would certainly be her husband. Marie felt that her limbs could not work nor her tongue speak were it not for this one drop of water in her cup.

And then, deeply meditating, La Mère Bauche hit upon a plan and herself communicated it to the capitaine over a second cup of coffee into which she poured a full teaspoonful more than the usual allowance of cognac. Why should not he, the capitaine himself, be the man to marry Marie Clavert?

It was a very startling proposal, the idea of matrimony for himself never having as yet entered into the capitaine's head at any period of his life; but La Mère Bauche did contrive to make it not altogether unacceptable. As to that matter of dowry she was prepared to be more than generous. She did love Marie well, and could find it in her heart to give her anything— anything except her son, her own Adolphe. What she proposed was this. Adolphe, himself, would never keep the baths. If the capitaine would take Marie for his wife, Marie, Madame Bauche declared, should be the mistress after her death; subject of course to certain settlements as to Adolphe's pecuniary interests.

The plan was discussed a thousand times, and at last so far brought to bear that Marie was made acquainted with it—

having been called in to sit in presence with La Mère Bauche and her future proposed husband. The poor girl manifested no disgust to the stiff ungainly lover whom they assigned to her,—who through his whole frame was in appearance almost as wooden as his own leg. On the whole, indeed, Marie liked the capitaine, and felt that he was her friend; and in her country such marriages were not uncommon. The capitaine was perhaps a little beyond the age at which a man might usually be thought justified in demanding the services of a young girl as his nurse and wife, but then Marie of herself had so little to give—except her youth, and beauty, and goodness.

But yet she could not absolutely consent; for was she not absolutely pledged on her own Adolphe? And therefore, when the great pecuniary advantages were, one by one, displayed before her, and when La Mère Bauche, as a last argument, informed her that as wife of the capitaine she would be regarded as a second mistress in the establishment and not as a servant,—she could only burst out into tears, and say that she did not know.

"I will be very kind to you," said the capitaine; "as kind as a man can be."

Marie took his hard withered hand and kissed it; and then looked up into his face with beseeching eyes which were not without avail upon his heart.

"We will not press her now," said the capitaine. "There is time enough."

But let his heart be touched ever so much, one thing was certain. It could not be permitted that she should marry Adolphe. To that view of the matter he had given in his unrestricted adhesion; nor could he by any means withdraw it without losing altogether his position in the establishment of Madame Bauche. Nor indeed did his conscience tell him that such a marriage should be permitted. That would be too much. If every pretty girl were allowed to marry the first young man that might fall in love with her, what would the world come to?

And it soon appeared that there was not time enough—that the time was growing very scant. In three months Adolphe would be back. And if everything was not arranged by that time, matters might still go astray.

And then Madame Bauche asked her final question: "You do not think, do you, that you can ever marry Adolphe?" And as she asked it the accustomed terror of her green spectacles magnified itself tenfold. Marie could only answer by another burst of tears.

The affair was at last settled among them. Marie said that she would consent to marry the capitaine when she should hear from Adolphe's own mouth that he, Adolphe, loved her no longer. She declared with many tears that her vows and pledges prevented her from promising more than this. It was not her fault, at any rate not now, that she loved her lover. It was not her fault,—not now at least—that she was bound by these pledges. When she heard from his own mouth that he had discarded her, then she would marry the capitaine—or indeed sacrifice herself in any other way that La Mère Bauche might desire. What would anything signify then?

Madame Bauche's spectacles remained unmoved; but not her heart. Marie, she told the capitaine, should be equal to herself in the establishment, when once she was entitled to be called Madame Campan, and she should be to her quite as a daughter. She should have her cup of coffee every evening, and dine at the big table, and wear a silk gown at church, and the servants should all call her Madame; a great career should be open to her, if she would only give up her foolish girlish childish love for Adolphe. And all these great promises were repeated to Marie by the capitaine.

But nevertheless there was but one thing in the whole world which in Marie's eyes was of any value; and that one thing was the heart of Adolphe Bauche. Without that she would be nothing; with that,—with that assured, she could wait patiently till doomsday.

Letters were written to Adolphe during all these eventful doings; and a letter came from him saying that he greatly valued Marie's love, but that as it had been clearly proved to him that their marriage would be neither for her advantage, nor for his, he was willing to give it up. He consented to her marriage with the capitaine, and expressed his gratitude to his mother for the immediate pecuniary advantages which she had held out to him. Oh, Adolphe, Adolphe! But, alas, alas! is not such the way of most men's hearts—and of the hearts of some women?

This letter was read to Marie, but it had no more effect upon her than would have had some dry legal document. In those days and in those places men and women did not depend much upon letters; nor when they were written, was there expressed in them much of heart or of feeling. Marie would understand, as she was well aware, the glance of Adolphe's eye and the tone of Adolphe's voice; she would perceive at once from them what her lover really meant, what he wished, what in the innermost corner of his heart he really desired that she should do. But from that stiff constrained written document she could understand nothing.

It was agreed therefore that Adolphe should return, and that she would accept her fate from his mouth. The capitaine, who knew more of human nature than did poor Marie, felt tolerably sure of his bride. Adolphe, who had seen something of the world, would not care very much for the girl of his own valley. Money and pleasure, and some little position in the world would soon wean him from his love; and then Marie would accept her destiny—as other girls in the same position had done since the French world began.

And now it was the evening before Adolphe's expected arrival. La Mère Bauche was discussing the matter with the capitaine over the usual cup of coffee. Madame Bauche had of late become rather nervous on the matter, thinking that they had been somewhat rash in acceding so much to Marie. It seemed to her that it was absolutely now left to the two young lovers to say whether or no they would have each other or not. Now nothing on earth could be further from Madame Bauche's intention than this. Her decree and resolve was to heap down blessings on all persons concerned—provided always that she could have her own way; but, provided she did not have her own way, to heap down,—anything but blessings. She had her code of morality in this matter. She would do good if possible to everybody around her. But she would not on any score be induced to consent that Adolphe should marry Marie Clavert. Should that be in the wind she would rid the house of Marie, of the capitaine, and even of Adolphe himself.

She had become therefore somewhat querulous, and self-opinionated in her discussions with her friend.

"I don't know," she said on the evening in question; "I don't know. It may be all right; but if Adolphe turns against me, what are we to do then?"

"Mère Bauche," said the capitaine, sipping his coffee and puffing out the smoke of his cigar, "Adolphe will not turn against us." It had been somewhat remarked by many that the capitaine was more at home in the house, and somewhat freer in his manner of talking with Madame Bauche, since this matrimonial alliance had been on the tapis than he had ever been before. La Mère herself observed it, and did not quite like it; but how could she prevent it now? When the capitaine was once married she would make him know his place, in spite of all her promises to Marie.

"But if he says he likes the girl?" continued Madame Bauche.

"My friend, you may be sure that he will say nothing of the kind. He has not been away two years without seeing girls as pretty as Marie. And then you have his letter."

"That is nothing, capitaine; he would eat his letter as quick as you would eat an omelet *aux fines herbes*." Now the capitaine was especially quick over an omelet *aux fines herbes*.

"And, Mère Bauche, you also have the purse; he will know that he cannot eat that, except with your good will."

"Ah!" exclaimed Madame Bauche, "poor lad! He has not a sous in the world unless I give it to him." But it did not seem that this reflection was in itself displeasing to her.

"Adolphe will now be a man of the world," continued the capitaine. "He will know that it does not do to throw away everything for a pair of red lips. That is the folly of a boy, and Adolphe will be no longer a boy. Believe me, Mère Bauche, things will be right enough."

"And then we shall have Marie sick and ill and half dying on our hands," said Madame Bauche.

This was not flattering to the capitaine, and so he felt it. "Perhaps so, perhaps not," he said. "But at any rate she will get over it. It is a malady which rarely kills young women—especially when another alliance awaits them."

"Bah!" said Madame Bauche; and in saying that word she avenged herself for the too great liberty which the capitaine had lately taken. He shrugged his shoulders, took a pinch of snuff, and uninvited helped himself to a teaspoonful of cognac. Then the conference ended, and on the next morning before breakfast Adolphe Bauche arrived.

On that morning poor Marie hardly knew how to bear herself. A month or two back, and even up to the last day or two, she had felt a sort of confidence that Adolphe would be true to her; but the nearer came that fatal day the less strong was the confidence of the poor girl. She knew that those two long-headed, aged counsellors were plotting against her happiness, and she felt that she could hardly dare hope for success with such terrible foes opposed to her. On the evening before the day Madame Bauche had met her in the passages, and kissed her as she wished her good night. Marie knew little about sacrifices, but she felt that it was a sacrificial kiss.

In those days a sort of diligence with the mails for Olette passed through Prades early in the morning, and a conveyance was sent from Vernet to bring Adolphe to the baths. Never was prince or princess expected with more anxiety. Madame Bauche was up and dressed long before the hour, and was heard to say five several times that she was sure he would not come. The capitaine was out and on the high road, moving about with his wooden leg, as perpendicular as a lamp-post and almost as black. Marie also was up, but nobody had seen her. She was up and had been out about the place before any of them were stirring; but now that the world was on the move she lay hidden like a hare in its form.

And then the old char-à-banc clattered up to the door, and Adolphe jumped out of it into his mother's arms. He was fatter and fairer than she had last seen him, had a larger beard, was more fashionably clothed, and certainly looked more like a man. Marie also saw him out of her little window, and she thought that he looked like a god. Was it probable, she said to herself, that one so godlike would still care for her?

The mother was delighted with her son, who rattled away quite at his ease. He shook hands very cordially with the capitaine—of whose intended alliance with his own sweetheart he had been informed, and then as he entered the house with his hand under his mother's arm, he asked one question about her. "And where is Marie?" said he. "Marie! oh upstairs; you shall see her after breakfast," said La Mère Bauche. And so they entered the house, and went in to breakfast among the guests. Everybody had heard something of the story, and they were all on the alert to see the young man whose love or want of love was considered to be of so much importance.

"You will see that it will be all right," said the capitaine, carrying his head very high.

"I think so, I think so," said La Mère Bauche, who, now that the capitaine was right, no longer desired to contradict him.

"I know that it will be all right," said the capitaine. "I told you that Adolphe would return a man; and he is a man. Look at him; he does not care this for Marie Clavert"; and the capitaine, with much eloquence in his motion, pitched over a neighbouring wall a small stone which he held in his hand.

And then they all went to breakfast with many signs of outward joy. And not without some inward joy; for Madame Bauche thought she saw that her son was cured of his love. In the mean time Marie sat up stairs still afraid to show herself.

"He has come," said a young girl, a servant in the house, running up to the door of Marie's room.

"Yes," said Marie; "I could see that he has come."

"And, oh, how beautiful he is!" said the girl, putting her hands together and looking up to the ceiling. Marie in her heart of hearts wished that he was not half so beautiful, as then her chance of having him might be greater.

"And the company are all talking to him as though he were the préfet," said the girl.

"Never mind who is talking to him," said Marie; "go away,

and leave me—you are wanted for your work." Why before this was he not talking to her? Why not, if he were really true to her? Alas, it began to fall upon her mind that he would be false! And what then? What should she do then? She sat still gloomily, thinking of that other spouse that had been promised to her.

As speedily after breakfast as was possible Adolphe was invited to a conference in his mother's private room. She had much debated in her own mind whether the capitaine should be invited to this conference or no. For many reasons she would have wished to exclude him. She did not like to teach her son that she was unable to manage her own affairs, and she would have been well pleased to make the capitaine understand that his assistance was not absolutely necessary to her. But then she had an inward fear that her green spectacles would not now be as efficacious on Adolphe, as they had once been, in old days, before he had seen the world and become a man. It might be necessary that her son, being a man should be opposed by a man. So the capitaine was invited to the conference.

What took place there need not be described at length. The three were closeted for two hours, at the end of which time they came forth together. The countenance of Madame Bauche was serene and comfortable; her hopes of ultimate success ran higher than ever. The face of the capitaine was masked, as are always the faces of great diplomatists; he walked placid and upright, raising his wooden leg with an ease and skill that was absolutely marvellous. But poor Adolphe's brow was clouded. Yes, poor Adolphe! for he was poor in spirit. He had pledged himself to give up Marie, and to accept the liberal allowance which his mother tendered him; but it remained for him now to communicate these tidings to Marie herself.

"Could not you tell her?" he had said to his mother, with very little of that manliness in his face on which his mother now so prided herself. But La Mère Bauche explained to him that it was a part of the general agreement that Marie was to hear his decision from his own mouth.

"But you need not regard it," said the capitaine, with the most indifferent air in the world. "The girl expects it. Only she has some childish idea that she is bound till you yourself release her. I don't think she will be troublesome." Adolphe at that moment did feel that he should have liked to kick the capitaine out of his mother's house.

And where should the meeting take place? In the hall of the bath-house, suggested Madame Bauche; because, as she observed, they could walk round and round, and nobody ever went there at that time of day. But to this Adolphe objected; it would be so cold and dismal and melancholy.

The capitaine thought that Mère Bauche's little parlour was the place; but La Mère herself did not like this. They might be overheard, as she well knew; and she guessed that the meeting would not conclude without some sobs that would certainly be bitter and might perhaps be loud.

"Send her up to the grotto, and I will follow her," said Adolphe. On this therefore they agreed. Now the grotto was a natural excavation in a high rock, which stood precipitously upright over the establishment of the baths. A steep zigzag path with almost never-ending steps had been made along the face of the rock from a little flower garden attached to the house which lay immediately under the mountain. Close along the front of the hotel ran a little brawling river, leaving barely room for a road between it and the door; over this there was a wooden bridge leading to the garden, and some two or three hundred yards from the bridge began the steps by which the ascent was made to the grotto.

When the season was full and the weather perfectly warm the place was much frequented. There was a green table in it, and four or five deal chairs; a green garden seat also was there, which however had been removed into the innermost back corner of the excavation, as its hinder legs were somewhat at fault. A wall about two feet high ran along the face of it, guarding its occupants from the precipice. In fact it was no grotto, but a little chasm in the rock, such as we often see up above our heads in rocky valleys, and which by means of these steep steps had been turned into a source of exercise and amusement for the visitors at the hotel.

Standing at the wall one could look down into the garden,

and down also upon the shining slate roof of Madame Bauche's house; and to the left might be seen the sombre silent snow-capped top of stern old Canigou, king of mountains among those Eastern Pyrenees.

And so Madame Bauche undertook to send Marie up to the grotto, and Adolphe undertook to follow her thither. It was now spring; and though the winds had fallen and the snow was no longer lying on the lower peaks, still the air was fresh and cold, and there was no danger that any of the few guests at the establishment would visit the place.

"Make her put on her cloak, Mère Bauche," said the capitaine, who did not wish that his bride should have a cold in her head on their wedding-day. La Mère Bauche pished and pshawed, as though she were not minded to pay any attention to recommendations on such subjects from the capitaine. But nevertheless when Marie was seen slowly to creep across the little bridge about fifteen minutes after this time, she had a handkerchief on her head, and was closely wrapped in a dark brown cloak.

Poor Marie herself little heeded the cold fresh air, but she was glad to avail herself of any means by which she might hide her face. When Madame Bauche sought her out in her own little room, and with a smiling face and kind kiss bade her go to the grotto, she knew, or fancied that she knew that it was all over.

"He will tell you all the truth—how it all is," said La Mère. "We will do all we can, you know, to make you happy, Marie. But you must remember what Monsieur le Curé told us the other day. In this vale of tears we cannot have everything; as we shall have some day, when our poor wicked souls have been purged of all their wickedness. Now go, dear, and take your cloak."

"Yes, maman."

"And Adolphe will come to you. And try and behave well, like a sensible girl."

"Yes, maman,"—and so she went, bearing on her brow another sacrificial kiss—and bearing in her heart such an unutterable load of woe!

Adolphe had gone out of the house before her; but standing in the stable yard, well within the gate so that she should not see him, he watched her slowly crossing the bridge and mounting the first flight of the steps. He had often seen her tripping up those stairs, and had, almost as often, followed her with his quicker feet. And she, when she would hear him, would run; and then he would catch her breathless at the top, and steal kisses from her when all power of refusing them had been robbed from her by her efforts at escape. There was no such running now, no such following, no thought of such kisses.

As for him, he would fain have skulked off and shirked the interview had he dared. But he did not dare; so he waited there, out of heart, for some ten minutes, speaking a word now and then to the bath-man, who was standing by, just to show that he was at his ease. But the bath-man knew that he was not at his ease. Such would-be lies as those rarely achieve deception;— are rarely believed. And then, at the end of the ten minutes, with steps as slow as Marie's had been, he also ascended to the grotto.

Marie had watched him from the top, but so that she herself should not be seen. He however had not once lifted up his head to look for her; but, with eyes turned to the ground had plodded his way up to the cave. When he entered she was standing in the middle, with her eyes downcast, and her hands clasped before her. She was retired some way from the wall, so that no eyes might possibly see her but those of her false lover. There she stood when he entered, striving to stand motionless, but trembling like a leaf in every limb.

It was only when he reached the top step that he made up his mind how he would behave. Perhaps after all, the capitaine was right; perhaps she would not mind it.

"Marie," said he, with a voice that attempted to be cheerful; "this is an odd place to meet in after such a long absence," and he held out his hand to her. But only his hand! He offered her no salute. He did not even kiss her cheek as a brother would have done! Of the rules of the outside world it must be remembered that poor Marie knew but little. He had been a brother to her, before he had become her lover.

But Marie took his hand saying, "Yes, it has been very long."

"And now that I have come back," he went on to say, "It seems that we are all in a confusion together. I never knew such a piece of work. However, it is all for the best, I suppose."

"Perhaps so," said Marie still trembling violently, and still looking down upon the ground. And then there was silence between them for a minute or so.

"I tell you what it is, Marie," said Adolphe at last, dropping her hand and making a great effort to get through the work before him. "I am afraid we two have been very foolish. Don't you think we have now? It seems quite clear that we can never get ourselves married. Don't you see it in that light?"

Marie's head turned round and round with her, but she was not of the fainting order. She took three steps backwards and leant against the wall of the cave. She also was trying to think how she might best fight her battle. Was there no chance for her? Could no eloquence, no love prevail? On her own beauty she counted but little; but might not prayers do something, and a reference to those old vows which had been so frequent, so eager, so solemnly pledged between them?

"Never get ourselves married!" she said, repeating his words. "Never, Adolphe? Can we never be married?"

"Upon my word, my dear girl, I fear not. You see my mother is so dead against it."

"But we could wait; could we not?"

"Ah, but that's just it, Marie. We cannot wait. We must decide now,—to-day. You see I can do nothing without money from her—and as for you, you see she won't even let you stay in the house unless you marry old Campan at once. He's a very good sort of fellow though, old as he is. And if you do marry him, why you see you'll stay here, and have it all your own way in everything. As for me, I shall come and see you all from time to time, and shall be able to push my way as I ought to do."

"Then, Adolphe, you wish me to marry the capitaine?"

"Upon my honour I think it is the best thing you can do; I do indeed."

"Oh, Adolphe!"

"What can I do for you, you know? Suppose I was to go down to my mother and tell her that I had decided to keep you myself, what would come of it? Look at it in that light, Marie."

"She could not turn you out—you her own son!"

"But she would turn you out; and deuced quick, too, I can assure you of that; I can, upon my honour."

"I should not care that," and she made a motion with her hand to show how indifferent she would be to such treatment as regarded herself. "Not that—; if I still had the promise of your love."

"But what would you do?"

"I would work. There are other houses besides that one," and she pointed to the slate roof of the Bauche establishment.

"And for me—I should not have a penny in the world," said the young man.

She came up to him and took his right hand between both of hers and pressed it warmly, oh, so warmly. "You would have my love," said she; "my deepest, warmest, best heart's love. I should want nothing more, nothing on earth, if I could still have yours." And she leaned against his shoulder and looked with all her eyes into his face.

"But, Marie; that's nonsense, you know."

"No, Adolphe; it is not nonsense. Do not let them teach you so. What does love mean, if it does not mean that? Oh, Adolphe, you do love me, you do love me; you do love me?"

"Yes;—I love you," he said slowly;—as though he would not have said it, if he could have helped it. And then his arm crept slowly round her waist, as though in that also he could not help himself.

"And do not I love you?" said the passionate girl. "Oh I do, so dearly; with all my heart, with all my soul. Adolphe, I so love you, that I cannot give you up. Have I not sworn to be yours; sworn, sworn a thousand times? How can I marry that man! Oh Adolphe, how can you wish that I should marry him?" And she clung to him, and looked at him, and besought him with her eyes.

"I shouldn't wish it;—only—" and then he paused. It was

hard to tell her that he was willing to sacrifice her to the old man because he wanted money from his mother.

"Only what! But, Adolphe, do not wish it at all! Have you not sworn that I should be your wife? Look here, look at this;" and she brought out from her bosom a little charm that he had given her in return for that cross. "Did you not kiss that when you swore before the figure of the virgin that I should be your wife? And do you not remember that I feared to swear too, because your mother was so angry; and then you made me? After that, Adolphe! Oh, Adolphe! Tell me that I may have some hope. I will wait; oh, I will wait so patiently."

He turned himself away from her and walked backwards and forwards uneasily through the grotto. He did love her;—love her as such men do love sweet, pretty girls. The warmth of her hand, the affection of her touch, the pure bright passion of her tear-laden eye had reawakened what power of love there was within him. But what was he to do? Even if he were willing to give up the immediate golden hopes which his mother held out to him, how was he to begin, and then how carry out his work of self-devotion? Marie would be turned away, and he would be left a victim in the hands of his mother, and of that stiff, wooden-legged militaire;—a penniless victim, left to mope about the place without a grain of influence or a morsel of pleasure.

"But what can we do?" he exclaimed again, as he once more met Marie's searching eye.

"We can be true and honest, and we can wait," she said, coming close up to him and taking hold of his arm. "I do not fear it; and she is not my mother, Adolphe. You need not fear your own mother."

"Fear; no of course I don't fear. But I don't see how the very devil we can manage it."

"Will you let me tell her that I will not marry the capitaine; that I will not give up your promises; and then I am ready to leave the house?"

"It would do no good."

"It would do every good, Adolphe, if I had your promised word once more; if I could hear from your own voice one more tone of love. Do you not remember this place? It was here that you forced me to say that I loved you. It is here also that you will tell me that I have been deceived."

"It is not I that would deceive you," he said. "I wonder that you should be so hard upon me. God knows that I have trouble enough."

"Well; if I am a trouble to you, be it so. Be it as you wish," and she leaned back against the wall of the rock, and crossing her arms upon her breast looked away from him and fixed her eyes upon the sharp granite peaks of Canigou.

He again betook himself to walk backwards and forwards through the cave. He had quite enough of love for her to make him wish to marry her; quite enough, now, at this moment, to make the idea of her marriage with the capitaine very distasteful to him; enough probably to make him become a decently good husband to her, should fate enable him to marry her; but not enough to enable him to support all the punishment which would be the sure effects of his mother's displeasure. Besides, he had promised his mother that he would give up Marie;—had entirely given in his adhesion to that plan of the marriage with the capitaine. He had owned that the path of life as marked out for him by his mother was the one which it behoved him, as a man, to follow. It was this view of his duties as a man which had been specially urged on him with all the capitaine's eloquence. And old Campan had entirely succeeded. It is so easy to get the assent of such young men, so weak in mind and so weak in pocket, when the arguments are backed by a promise of two thousand francs a year.

"I'll tell you what I'll do," at last he said. "I'll get my mother by herself, and will ask her to let the matter remain as it is for the present."

"Not if it be a trouble, M. Adolphe;" and the proud girl still held her hands upon her bosom, and still looked towards the mountain.

"You know what I mean, Marie. You can understand how she and the capitaine are worrying me."

"But tell me, Adolphe, do you love me?"

"You know I love you, only—"

"And you will not give me up?"

"I will ask my mother. I will try and make her yield."

Marie could not feel that she received much confidence from her lover's promise; but still, even that, weak and unsteady as it was, even that was better than absolute fixed rejection. So she thanked him, promised him with tears in her eyes that she would always, always be faithful to him, and then bade him go down to the house. She would follow, she said, as soon as his passing had ceased to be observed.

Then she looked at him as though she expected some sign of renewed love. But no such sign was vouchsafed to her. Now that she thirsted for the touch of his lip upon her cheek, it was denied to her. He did as she bade him; he went down, slowly loitering, by himself; and in about half an hour she followed him and unobserved crept to her chamber.

Again we will pass over what took place between the mother and the son; but late in that evening, after the guests had gone to bed, Marie received a message, desiring her to wait on Madame Bauche in a small salon which looked out from one end of the house. It was intended as a private sitting-room should any special stranger arrive who required such accommodation, and therefore was but seldom used. Here she found La Mère Bauche sitting in an arm-chair behind a small table on which stood two candles; and on a sofa against the wall sat Adolphe. The capitaine was not in the room.

"Shut the door, Marie, and come in and sit down," said Madame Bauche. It was easy to understand from the tone of her voice that she was angry and stern, in an unbending mood, and resolved to carry out to the very letter all the threats conveyed by those terrible spectacles.

Marie did as she was bid. She closed the door and sat down on the chair that was nearest to her.

"Marie," said La Mère Bauche—and the voice sounded fierce in the poor girl's ears, and an angry fire glimmered through the green glasses—"what is all this about that I hear? Do you dare to say that you hold my son bound to marry you?" And then the august mother paused for an answer.

But Marie had no answer to give. She looked suppliantly

towards her lover, as though beseeching him to carry on the fight for her. But if she could not do battle for herself, certainly he could not do it for her. What little amount of fighting he had had in him, had been thoroughly vanquished before her arrival.

"I will have an answer, and that immediately," said Madame Bauche. "I am not going to be betrayed into ignominy and disgrace by the object of my own charity. Who picked you out of the gutter, miss, and brought you up and fed you, when you would otherwise have gone to the foundling? And is this your gratitude for it all? You are not satisfied with being fed and clothed and cherished by me, but you must rob me of my son! Know this then, Adolphe shall never marry a child of charity such as you are."

Marie sat still, stunned by the harshness of these words. La Mère Bauche had often scolded her; indeed, she was given to much scolding; but she had scolded her as a mother may scold a child. And when this story of Marie's love first reached her ears, she had been very angry; but her anger had never brought her to such a pass as this. Indeed, Marie had not hitherto been taught to look at the matter in this light. No one had heretofore twitted her with eating the bread of charity. It had not occurred to her that on this account she was unfit to be Adolphe's wife. There, in that valley, they were all so nearly equal, that no idea of her own inferiority had ever pressed itself upon her mind. But now—!

When the voice ceased she again looked at him; but it was no longer with a beseeching look. Did he also altogether scorn her? That was now the inquiry which her eyes were called upon to make. No; she could not say that he did. It seemed to her that his energies were chiefly occupied in pulling to pieces the tassel of the sofa cushion.

"And now, miss, let me know at once whether this nonsense is to be over or not," continued La Mère Bauche; "and I will tell you at once, I am not going to maintain you here, in my house, to plot against our welfare and happiness. As Marie Clavert you shall not stay here. Capitaine Campan is willing to marry you; and as his wife I will keep my word to you, though you little deserve it. If you refuse to marry him, you must go. As to my son, he is there; and he will tell you now, in my presence, that he altogether declines the honour you propose for him."

And then she ceased, waiting for an answer, drumming the table with a wafer stamp which happened to be ready to her hand; but Marie said nothing. Adolphe had been appealed to; but Adolphe had not yet spoken.

"Well, miss?" said La Mère Bauche.

Then Marie rose from her seat, and walking round she touched Adolphe lightly on the shoulder. "Adolphe," she said, "it is for you to speak now. I will do as you bid me."

He gave a long sigh, looked first at Marie and then at his mother, shook himself slightly, and then spoke: "Upon my word, Marie, I think mother is right. It would never do for us to marry; it would not indeed."

"Then it is decided," said Marie, returning to her chair.

"And you will marry the capitaine?" said La Mère Bauche. Marie merely bowed her head in token of acquiescence.

"Then we are friends again. Come here, Marie, and kiss me. You must know that it is my duty to take care of my own son. But I don't want to be angry with you if I can help it; I don't indeed. When once you are Madame Campan, you shall be my own child; and you shall have any room in the house you like to choose—there!" And she once more imprinted a kiss on Marie's cold forehead.

How they all got out of the room, and off to their own chambers, I can hardly tell. But in five minutes from the time of this last kiss they were divided. La Mère Bauche had patted Marie, and smiled on her, and called her her dear good little Madame Campan, her young little mistress of the Hôtel Bauche; and had then got herself into her own room, satisfied with her own victory.

Nor must my readers be too severe on Madame Bauche. She had already done much for Marie Clavert; and when she found herself once more by her own bedside, she prayed to be forgiven for the cruelty which she felt that she had shown to the orphan. But in making this prayer, with her favourite crucifix in her hand and the little image of the Virgin before her, she pleaded her duty to her son. Was it not right, she asked the Virgin, that she should save her son from a bad marriage? And then she promised ever so much of recompense, both to the Virgin and to Marie; a new trousseau for each, with candles to the Virgin, with a gold watch and chain for Marie, as soon as she should be Marie Campan. She had been cruel; she acknowledged it. But at such a crisis was it not defensible? And then the recompense should be so full!

But there was one other meeting that night, very short indeed, but not the less significant. Not long after they had all separated just so long as to allow of the house being quiet, Adolphe, still sitting in his room, meditating on what the day had done for him, heard a low tap at his door. "Come in," he said, as men always do say; and Marie opening the door, stood just within the verge of his chamber. She had on her countenance neither the soft look of entreating love which she had worn up there in the grotto, nor did she appear crushed and subdued as she had done before his mother. She carried her head somewhat more erect than usual, and looked boldly out at him from under her soft eyelashes. There might still be love there, but it was love proudly resolving to quell itself. Adolphe as he looked at her, felt that he was afraid of her.

"It is all over then between us, M. Adolphe?" she said.

"Well, yes. Don't you think it had better be so, eh, Marie?"

"And this is the meaning of oaths and vows, sworn to each other so sacredly?"

"But, Marie, you heard what my mother said."

"Oh, sir! I have not come to ask you again to love me. Oh, no! I am not thinking of that. But this, this would be a lie if I kept it now; it would choke me if I wore it as that man's wife. Take it back;" and she tendered to him the little charm which she had always worn round her neck since he had given it to her. He took it abstractedly, without thinking what he did, and placed it on his dressing-table.

"And you," she continued, "can you still keep that cross?

Oh, no! you must give me back that. It would remind you too often of vows that were untrue."

"Marie," he said, "do not be so harsh to me."

"Harsh!" said she, "no; there has been enough of harshness. I would not be harsh to you, Adolphe. But give me the cross; it would prove a curse to you if you kept it."

He then opened a little box which stood upon the table, and taking out the cross gave it to her.

"And now good-bye," she said. "We shall have but little more to say to each other. I know this now, that I was wrong ever to have loved you. I should have been to you as one of the other poor girls in the house. But, oh! how was I to help it?" To this he made no answer, and she, closing the door softly, went back to her chamber. And thus ended the first day of Adolphe Bauche's return to his own house.

On the next morning the capitaine and Marie were formally betrothed. This was done with some little ceremony, in the presence of all the guests who were staying at the establishment, and with all manner of gracious acknowledgements of Marie's virtues. It seemed as though La Mère Bauche could not be courteous enough to her. There was no more talk of her being a child of charity; no more allusion now to the gutter. La Mère Bauche with her own hand brought her cake with a glass of wine after her betrothal was over, and patted her on the cheek, and called her her dear little Marie Campan. And then the capitaine was made up of infinite politeness, and the guests all wished her joy, and the servants of the house began to perceive that she was a person entitled to respect. How different was all this from the harsh attack that was made on her the preceding evening! Only Adolphe,—he alone kept aloof. Though he was present there he said nothing. He, and he only, offered no congratulations.

In the midst of all these gala doings Marie herself said little or nothing. La Mère Bauche perceived this, but she forgave it. Angrily as she had expressed herself at the idea of Marie's daring to love her son, she had still acknowledged within her own heart that such love had been natural. She could feel no pity for Marie as long as Adolphe was in danger; but now she knew how to pity her. So Marie was still petted and still encouraged, though she went through the day's work sullenly and in silence.

As to the capitaine it was all one to him. He was a man of the world. He did not expect that he should really be preferred, *con amore*, to a young fellow like Adolphe. But he did expect that Marie, like other girls, would do as she was bid; and that in a few days she would regain her temper and be reconciled to her life.

And then the marriage was fixed for a very early day; for as La Mère said, "What was the use of waiting? All their minds were made up now, and therefore the sooner the two were married the better. Did not the capitaine think so?"

The capitaine said that he did think so.

And then Marie was asked. It was all one to her, she said. Whatever Maman Bauche liked, that she would do; only she would not name a day herself. Indeed she would neither do nor say anything herself which tended in any way to a furtherance of these matrimonials. But then she acquiesced, quietly enough if not readily, in what other people did and said; and so the marriage was fixed for the day week after Adolphe's return.

The whole of that week passed much in the same way. The servants about the place spoke among themselves of Marie's perverseness, obstinacy, and ingratitude, because she would not look pleased, or answer Madame Bauche's courtesies with gratitude; but La Mère herself showed no signs of anger. Marie had yielded to her, and she required no more. And she remembered also the harsh words she had used to gain her purpose; and she reflected on all that Marie had lost. On these accounts she was forbearing and exacted nothing—nothing but that one sacrifice which was to be made in accordance to her wishes.

And it was made. They were married in the great salon, the dining-room, immediately after breakfast. Madame Bauche was dressed in a new puce silk dress and looked very magnificent on the occasion. She simpered and smiled, and looked gay even in spite of her spectacles; and as the ceremony was being performed, she held fast clutched in her hand the gold watch and chain which were intended for Marie as soon as ever the marriage should be completed.

The capitaine was dressed exactly as usual, only that all his clothes were new. Madame Bauche had endeavoured to persuade him to wear a blue coat; but he answered that such a change would not, he was sure, be to Marie's taste. To tell the truth, Marie would hardly have known the difference had he presented himself in scarlet vestments.

Adolphe, however, was dressed very finely, but he did not make himself prominent on the occasion. Marie watched him closely, though none saw that she did so; and of his garments she could have given an account with much accuracy—of his garments, ay! and of every look. "Is he a man," she said at last to herself, "that he can stand by and see all this?"

She too was dressed in silk. They had put on her what they pleased, and she bore the burden of her wedding finery without complaint and without pride. There was no blush on her face as she walked up to the table at which the priest stood, nor hesitation in her low voice as she made the necessary answers. She put her hand into that of the capitaine when required to do so; and when the ring was put on her finger she shuddered, but ever so slightly. No one observed it but La Mère Bauche. "In one week she will be used to it, and then we shall all be happy," said La Mère to herself. "And I,—I will be so kind to her!"

And so the marriage was completed, and the watch was at once given to Marie. "Thank you, maman," said she, as the trinket was fastened to her girdle. Had it been a pincushion that had cost three sous, it would have affected her as much.

And then there was cake, and wine, and sweetmeats; and after a few minutes Marie disappeared. For an hour or so the capitaine was taken up with the congratulations of his friends, and with the efforts necessary to the wearing of his new honours with an air of ease; but after that time he began to be uneasy because his wife did not come to him. At two or three in the afternoon he went to La Mère Bauche to complain. "This lackadaisical nonsense is no good," he said. "At any rate it is too late now. Marie had better come down among us and show herself satisfied with her husband."

But Madame Bauche took Marie's part. "You must not be too hard on Marie," she said. "She has gone through a good deal this week past, and is very young; whereas, capitaine, you are not very young."

The capitaine merely shrugged his shoulders. In the mean time Mère Bauche went up to visit her protégé in her own room, and came down with a report that she was suffering from a headache. She could not appear at dinner, Madame Bauche said; but would make one at the little party which was to be given in the evening. With this the capitaine was forced to be content.

The dinner therefore went on quietly without her, much as it did on other ordinary days. And then there was a little time of vacancy, during which the gentlemen drank their coffee and smoked their cigars at the café, talking over the event that had taken place that morning, and the ladies brushed their hair and added some ribbon or some brooch to their usual apparel. Twice during this time did Madame Bauche go up to Marie's room with offers to assist her. "Not yet, maman; not quite yet," said Marie piteously through her tears, and then twice did the green spectacles leave the room, covering eyes which also were not dry. Ah! what had she done? What had she dared to take upon herself to do? She could not undo it now.

And then it became quite dark in the passages and out of doors, and the guests assembled in the salon. La Mère came in and out three or four times, uneasy in her gait and unpleasant in her aspect, and everybody began to see that things were wrong. "She is ill, I am afraid," said one. "The excitement has been too much," said a second; "and he is so old," whispered a third. And the capitaine stalked about erect on his wooden leg, taking snuff, and striving to look indifferent; but he also was uneasy in his mind.

Presently La Mère came in again, with a quicker step than before, and whispered something, first to Adolphe and then to the capitaine, whereupon they both followed her out of the room.

"Not in her chamber?" said Adolphe.

"Then she must be in yours," said the capitaine.

"She is in neither," said La Mère Bauche, with her sternest voice; "nor is she in the house."

And now there was no longer an affectation of indifference on the part of any of them. They were anything but indifferent. The capitaine was eager in his demands that the matter should still be kept secret from the guests. She had always been romantic, he said, and had now gone out to walk by the river-side. They three and the old bath-man would go out and look for her. "But it is pitch dark," said La Mère Bauche.

"We will take lanterns," said the capitaine. And so they sallied forth with creeping steps over the gravel, so that they might not be heard by those within, and proceeded to search for the young wife.

"Marie! Marie!" said La Mère Bauche, in piteous accents; "do come to me; pray do!"

"Hush!" said the capitaine. "They'll hear you if you call." He could not endure that the world should learn that a marriage with him had been so distasteful to Marie Clavert.

"Marie, dear Marie!" called Madame Bauche, louder than before, quite regardless of the capitaine's feelings; but no Marie answered. In her innermost heart now did La Mère Bauche wish that this cruel marriage had been left undone.

Adolphe was foremost with his lamp, but he hardly dared to look in the spot where he felt that it was most likely that she should have taken refuge. How could he meet her again, alone, in that grotto? Yet he alone of the four was young. It was clearly for him to ascend. "Marie!" he shouted, "are you there?" as he slowly began the long ascent of the steps.

But he had hardly begun to mount when a whirring sound struck his ear, and he felt that the air near him was moved; and then there was a crash upon the lower platform of rock, and a moan, repeated twice but so faintly, and a rustle of silk, and a slight struggle somewhere as he knew within twenty paces of him; and then all was again quiet and still in the night air.

"What was that?" asked the capitaine in a harsh voice. He made his way half across the little garden, and he also was within forty or fifty yards of the flat rock. But Adolphe was unable to answer him. He had fainted and the lamp had fallen from his hands, and rolled to the bottom of the steps.

But the capitaine, though even his heart was all but quenched within him, had still strength enough to make his way up to the rock; and there, holding the lantern above his eyes, he saw all that was left for him to see of his bride.

As for La Mère Bauche, she never again sat at the head of that table—never again dictated to guests—never again laid down laws for the management of any one. A poor bedridden old woman, she lay there in her house at Vernet for some seven tedious years, and then was gathered to her fathers.

As for the capitaine—but what matters? He was made of sterner stuff. What matters either the fate of such a one as Adolphe Bauche?

The Journey to Panama

There is perhaps no form of life in which men and women of the present day frequently find themselves for a time existing, so unlike their customary conventional life, as that experienced on board the large ocean steamers. On the voyages so made, separate friendships are formed and separate enmities are endured. Certain lines of temporary politics are originated by the energetic, and intrigues, generally innocent in their conclusions, are carried on with the keenest spirit by those to whom excitement is necessary; whereas the idle and torpid sink into insignificance and general contempt,—as it is their lot to do on board ship as in other places. But the enjoyments and activity of such a life do not display themselves till the third or fourth day of the voyage. The men and women at first regard each with distrust and ill-concealed dislike. They by no means anticipate the strong feelings which are to arise, and look forward to ten, fifteen, or twenty days of gloom or sea-sickness. Sea-sickness disappears, as a general condition, on the evening of the second day, and the gloom about noon on the fourth. Then the men begin to think that the women are not so ugly, vulgar, and insipid; and the women drop their monosyllables, discontinue the close adherence to their own niches, which they first observed, and become affable, perhaps even beyond their wont on shore. And alliances spring up among the men themselves. On their first entrance to this new world, they generally regard each other with marked aversion, each thinking that those nearest to him are low fellows, or perhaps worse; but by the fourth day, if not sooner, every man has his two or three intimate friends with whom he talks and smokes, and to whom he communicates those peculiar politics, and perhaps intrigues, of his own voyage. The female friendships are slower in their growth, for the suspicion of women is perhaps stronger than that of men; but when grown they also are stronger, and exhibit themselves sometimes in instances of feminine affection.

But the most remarkable alliances are those made between

gentlemen and ladies. This is a matter of course on board ship quite as much as on shore, and it is of such an alliance that the present tale purports to tell the story. Such friendships, though they may be very dear, can seldom be very lasting. Though they may be full of sweet romance—for people become very romantic among the discomforts of a sea voyage—such romance is generally short-lived and delusive, and occasionally is dangerous.

There are several of these great ocean routes, of which, by the common consent, as it seems, of the world, England is the centre. There is the Great Eastern line, running from Southampton across the Bay of Biscay and up the Mediterranean. It crosses the Isthmus of Suez, and branches away to Australia, to India, to Ceylon, and to China. There is the great American line, traversing the Atlantic to New York and Boston with the regularity of clockwork. The voyage here is so much a matter of every-day routine, that romance has become scarce upon the route. There are one or two other North American lines, perhaps open to the same objection. Then there is the line of packets to the African coast—very romantic as I am given to understand; and there is the great West-Indian route, to which the present little history is attached—great, not on account of our poor West Indian Islands, which cannot at the present moment make anything great, but because it spreads itself out from thence to Mexico and Cuba, to Guiana and the republics of Grenada and Venezuela, to Central America, the Isthmus of Panama, and from thence to California, Vancouver's Island, Peru and Chili.

It may be imagined how various are the tribes which leave the shores of Great Britain by this route. There are Frenchmen for the French sugar islands, as a rule not very romantic; there are old Spaniards, Spaniards of Spain, seeking to renew their fortunes amidst the ruins of their former empire; and new Spaniards—Spaniards, that is, of the American republics, who speak Spanish, but are unlike the Don both in manners and physiognomy—men and women with a touch perhaps of Indian blood, very keen after dollars, and not much given to the graces of life. There are Dutchmen too, and Danes, going out to their own islands. There are citizens of the stars and stripes, who find their way everywhere—and, alas! perhaps, now also citizens of the new Southern flag, with the palmetto leaf.[9] And there are Englishmen of every shade and class, and Englishwomen also.

It is constantly the case that women are doomed to make the long voyage alone. Some are going out to join their husbands, some to find a husband, some few peradventure to leave a husband. Girls who have been educated at home in England, return to their distant homes across the Atlantic, and others follow their relatives who have gone before them as pioneers into a strange land. It must not be supposed that these females absolutely embark in solitude, putting their feet upon the deck without the aid of any friendly arm. They are generally consigned to some prudent elder, and appear as they first show themselves on the ship to belong to a party. But as often as not their real loneliness shows itself after a while. The prudent elder is not, perhaps, congenial; and by the evening of the fourth day a new friendship is created.

Not a long time since such a friendship was formed under the circumstances which I am now about to tell. A young man— not very young, for he had turned his thirtieth year, but still a young man—left Southampton by one of the large West Indian steam-boats, purposing to pass over the Isthmus of Panama, and thence up to California and Vancouver's Island. It would be too long to tell the cause which led to these distant voyagings. Suffice to say, it was not the accursed hunger after gold—*auri sacra fames* —which so took him; nor had he any purpose of permanently settling himself in those distant colonies of Great Britain. He was at the time a widower, and perhaps his home was bitter to him without the young wife whom he had early lost. As he stepped on board he was accompanied by a gentleman some fifteen years his senior, who was to be the companion of his sleeping apartment as far as St. Thomas. The two had been introduced to each other, and therefore appeared as friends on board the *Serrapiqui*; but their acquaintance had commenced in Southampton, and my hero, Ralph Forrest by name, was alone in the world as he stood looking over the side of the ship at the retreating shores of Hampshire.

"I say, old fellow, we'd better see about our places," said his new friend, slapping him on his back. Mr. Matthew Morris was an old traveller, and knew how to become intimate with his temporary allies at a very short notice. A long course of travelling had knocked all bashfulness out of him, and when he had a mind to do so he could make any man his brother in half-an-hour, and any woman his sister in ten minutes.

"Places? what places?" said Forrest.

"A pretty fellow you are to go to California. If you don't look sharper than that you'll get little to drink and nothing to eat till you come back again. Don't you know the ship's as full as ever she can hold?"

Forrest acknowledged that she was full.

"There are places at table for about a hundred, and we have a hundred and thirty on board. As a matter of course those who don't look sharp will have to scramble. However I've put cards on the plates and taken the seats. We had better go down and see that none of these Spanish fellows oust us." So Forrest descended after his friend, and found that the long tables were already nearly full of expectant dinner-eaters. When he took his place a future neighbour informed him, not in the most gracious voice, that he was encroaching on a lady's seat; and when he immediately attempted to leave that which he held, Mr. Matthew Morris forbade him to do so. Thus a little contest arose, which, however, happily was brought to a close without bloodshed. The lady was not present at the moment, and the grumpy gentleman agreed to secure for himself a vacant seat on the other side.

For the first three days the lady did not show herself. The grumpy gentleman, who, as Forrest afterwards understood, was the owner of stores in Bridgetown, Barbadoes, had other ladies with him also. First came forth his daughter, creeping down to dinner on the second day, declaring that she would be unable to eat a morsel, and prophesying that she would be forced to retire in five minutes. On this occasion, however, she agreeably surprised herself and her friends. Then came the grumpy gentleman's wife, and the grumpy gentleman's wife's brother—on whose constitution the sea seemed to have an effect quite as violent as on that of the ladies; and lastly, at breakfast on the fourth day, appeared Miss Viner, and took her place as Mr. Forrest's neighbour at his right hand.

He had seen her before on deck, as she lay on one of the benches, vainly endeavouring to make herself comfortable, and had remarked to his companion that she was very unattractive and almost ugly. Dear young ladies, it is thus that men always speak of you when they first see you on board ship! She was disconsolate, sick at heart, and ill at ease in body also. She did not like the sea. She did not in the least like the grumpy gentleman, in whose hands she was placed. She did not especially like the grumpy gentleman's wife; and she altogether hated the grumpy gentleman's daughter, who was the partner of her berth. That young lady had been very sick and very selfish; and Miss Viner had been very sick also, and perhaps equally selfish. They might have been angels, and yet have hated each other under such circumstances. It was no wonder that Mr. Forrest thought her ugly as she twisted herself about on the broad bench, vainly striving to be comfortable.

"She'll brighten up wonderfully before we're in the tropics," said Mr. Morris. "And you won't find her so bad then. It's she that is to sit next you."

"Heaven forbid!" said Forrest. But, nevertheless, he was very civil to her when she did come down on the fourth morning. On board the West Indian Packets, the world goes down to its meals. In crossing between Liverpool and the States, the world goes up to them.

Miss Viner was by no means a very young lady. She also was nearly thirty. In guessing her age on board the ship the ladies said that she was thirty-six, but the ladies were wrong. She was an Irish woman, and when seen on shore, in her natural state, and with all her wits about her, was by no means without attraction. She was bright-eyed, with a clear dark skin, and good teeth; her hair was of a dark brown and glossy, and there was a touch of feeling and also of humour about her mouth, which would have saved her from Mr. Forrest's ill-considered criticism, had he first met her under more favourable circumstances.

"You'll see a good deal of her," Mr. Morris said to him, as they began to prepare themselves for luncheon, by a cigar immediately after breakfast. "She's going across the Isthmus and down to Peru."

"How on earth do you know?"

"I pretty well know where they're all going by this time. Old Grumpy told me so. He has her in tow as far as St. Thomas, but knows nothing about her. He gives her up there to the captain. You'll have a chance of making yourself very agreeable as you run across with her to the Spanish main."

Mr. Forrest replied that he did not suppose he should know her much better than he did now; but he made no further remark as to her ugliness. She had spoken a word or two to him at table, and he had seen that her eyes were bright, and had found that her tone was sweet.

"I also am going to Panama," he said to her, on the morning of the fifth day. The weather at that time was very fine, and the October sun as it shone on them, while hour by hour they made more towards the South, was pleasant and genial. The big ship lay almost without motion on the bosom of the Atlantic, as she was driven through the waters at the rate of twelve miles per hour. All was as pleasant now as things can be on board a ship, and Forrest had forgotten that Miss Viner had seemed so ugly to him when he first saw her. At this moment, as he spoke to her, they were running through the Azores, and he had been assisting her with his field-glass to look for orange-groves on their sloping shores, orange-groves they had not succeeded in seeing, but their failure had not disturbed their peace.

"I also am going to Panama."

"Are you, indeed?" said she. "Then I shall not feel so terribly alone and disconsolate. I have been looking forward with such fear to that journey on from St. Thomas."

"You shall not be disconsolate, if I can help it," he said. "I am not much of a traveller myself, but what I can do I will."

"Oh, thank you!"

"It is a pity Mr. Morris is not going on with you. He's at

home everywhere, and knows the way across the Isthmus as well as he does down Regent Street."

"Your friend, you mean?"

"My friend, if you call him so; and indeed I hope he is, for I like him. But I don't know more of him than I do of you. I also am as much alone as you are. Perhaps more so."

"But," she said, "a man never suffers in being alone."

"Oh! does he not? Don't think me uncivil, Miss Viner, if I say that you may be mistaken in that. You feel your own shoe when it pinches, but do not realize the tight boot of your neighbour."

"Perhaps not," said she. And then there was a pause, during which she pretended to look again for the orange-groves. "But there are worse things, Mr. Forrest, than being alone in the world. It is often a woman's lot to wish that she were let alone." Then she left him and retreated to the side of the grumpy gentleman's wife, feeling perhaps that it might be prudent to discontinue a conversation, which, seeing that Mr. Forrest was quite a stranger to her, was becoming particular.

"You're getting on famously, my dear," said the lady from Barbadoes.

"Pretty well, thank you, ma'am," said Miss Viner.

"Mr. Forrest seems to be making himself quite agreeable. I tell Amelia,"—Amelia was the young lady to whom in their joint cabin Miss Viner could not reconcile herself—"I tell Amelia that she is wrong not to receive attentions from gentlemen on board ship. If it is not carried too far," and she put great emphasis on the "too far"—"I see no harm in it."

"Nor I, either," said Miss Viner.

"But then Amelia is so particular."

"The best way is to take such things as they come," said Miss Viner,—perhaps meaning that such things never did come in the way of Amelia. "If a lady knows what she is about she need not fear a gentleman's attentions."

"That's just what I tell Amelia; but then, my dear, she has not had so much experience as you and I."

Such being the amenities which passed between Miss Viner

and the prudent lady who had her in charge, it was not wonderful that the former should feel ill at ease with her own "party", as the family of the Grumpy Barbadian was generally considered to be by those on board.

"You're getting along like a house on fire with Miss Viner," said Matthew Morris, to his young friend.

"Not much fire I can assure you," said Forrest.

"She ain't so ugly as you thought her?"

"Ugly!—no; she's not ugly. I don't think I ever said she was. But she is nothing particular as regards beauty."

"No; she won't be lovely for the next three days to come, I dare say. By the time you reach Panama, she'll be all that is perfect in woman. I know how these things go."

"Those sort of things don't go at all quickly with me," said Forrest, gravely. "Miss Viner is a very interesting young woman, and as it seems that her route and mine will be together for some time, it is well that we should be civil to each other. And the more so, seeing that the people she is with are not congenial to her."

"No; they are not. There is no young man with them. I generally observe that on board ship no one is congenial to unmarried ladies except unmarried men. It is a recognized nautical rule. Uncommon hot, isn't it? We are beginning to feel the tropical air. I shall go and cool myself with a cigar in the fiddle." The "fiddle" is a certain part of the ship devoted to smoking, and thither Mr. Morris betook himself. Forrest, however, did not accompany him, but going forward into the bow of the vessel, threw himself along upon the sail, and meditated on the loneliness of his life.

On board the *Serrapiqui*, the upper tier of cabins opened on to a long gallery, which ran round that part of the ship, immediately over the saloon, so that from thence a pleasant inspection could be made of the viands as they were being placed on the tables. The custom on board these ships is for two bells to ring preparatory to dinner, at an interval of half an hour. At the sound of the first, ladies would go to their cabins to adjust their toilets; but as dressing for dinner is not carried to an extreme at sea, these operations are generally over before the second bell, and the lady passengers would generally assemble in the balcony for some fifteen minutes before dinner. At first they would stand here alone, but by degrees they were joined by some of the more enterprising of the men, and so at last a kind of little drawing-room was formed. The cabins of Miss Viner's party opened to one side of this gallery, and that of Mr. Morris and Forrest on the other. Hitherto Forrest had been contented to remain on his own side, occasionally throwing a word across to the ladies on the other; but on this day he boldly went over as soon as he had washed his hands and took his place between Amelia and Miss Viner.

"We are dreadfully crowded here, ma'am," said Amelia.

"Yes, my dear, we are," said her mother. "But what can one do?"

"There's plenty of room in the ladies' cabin," said Miss Viner. Now if there be one place on board a ship more distasteful to ladies than another, it is the ladies' cabin. Mr. Forrest stood his ground, but it may be doubted whether he would have done so had he fully understood all that Amelia had intended.

Then the last bell rang. Mr. Grumpy gave his arm to Miss Grumpy.[10] The brother-in-law gave his arm to Amelia, and Forrest did the same to Miss Viner. She hesitated for a moment, and then took it, and by so doing transferred herself mentally and bodily from the charge of the prudent and married Mr. Grumpy to that of the perhaps imprudent, and certainly unmarried Mr. Forrest. She was wrong. A kind-hearted, motherly old lady from Jamaica, who had seen it all, knew that she was wrong, and wished that she could tell her so.

But there are things of this sort which kind-hearted old ladies cannot find it in their hearts to say. After all, it was only for the voyage. Perhaps Miss Viner was imprudent, but who in Peru would be the wiser? Perhaps, indeed, it was the world that was wrong, and not Miss Viner. *Honi soit qui mal y pense*, she said to herself, as she took his arm, and leaning on it, felt that she was no longer so lonely as she had been. On that day she allowed him to give her a glass of wine out of his decanter. "Hadn't you better take mine, Miss Viner?" asked Mr.

Grumpy, in a loud voice, but before he could be answered, the deed had been done.

"Don't go too fast, old fellow," Morris said to our hero that night, as they were walking the deck together before they turned in. "One gets into a hobble in such matters before one knows where one is."

"I don't think I have anything particular to fear," said Forrest.

"I dare say not, only keep your eyes open. Such haridans as Mrs. Grumpy allow any latitude to their tongues out in these diggings. You'll find that unpleasant tidings will be put on board the ship going down to Panama, and everybody's eye will be upon you." So warned, Mr. Forrest did put himself on his guard, and the next day and a half his intimacy with Miss Viner progressed but little. These were, probably, the dullest hours that he had on the whole voyage.

Miss Viner saw this and drew back. On the afternoon of that second day she walked a turn or two on deck with the weak brother-in-law, and when Mr. Forrest came near her, she applied herself to her book. She meant no harm; but if she were not afraid of what people might say, why should he be so? So she turned her shoulder towards him at dinner, and would not drink of his cup.

"Have some of mine, Miss Viner," said Mr. Grumpy, very loudly. But on that day Miss Viner drank no wine.

The sun sets quickly as one draws near to the tropics, and the day was already gone, and the dusk had come on, when Mr. Forrest walked out upon the deck that evening a little after six. But the night was beautiful and mild, and there was a hum of many voices from the benches. He was already uncomfortable, and sore with a sense of being deserted. There was but one person on board the ship that he liked, and why should he avoid her and be avoided? He soon perceived where she was standing. The Grumpy family had a bench to themselves, and she was opposite to it, on her feet, leaning against the side of the vessel. "Will you walk this evening, Miss Viner?" he asked.

"I think not," she answered.

"Then I shall persevere in asking till you are sure. It will do you good, for I have not seen you walking all day."

"Have you not? Then I will take a turn. Oh, Mr. Forrest, if you knew what it was to have to live with such people as those." And then, out of that, on that evening, there grew up between them something like the confidence of real friendship. Things were told such as none but friends do tell to one another, and warm answering words were spoken such as the sympathy of friendship produces. Alas, they were both foolish; for friendship and sympathy should have deeper roots.

She told him all her story. She was going out to Peru to be married to a man who was nearly twenty years her senior. It was a long engagement, of ten years' standing. When first made, it was made as being contingent on certain circumstances. An option of escaping from it had then been given to her, but now there was no longer an option. He was rich, and she was penniless. He had even paid her passage-money and her outfit. She had not at last given way and taken these irrevocable steps till her only means of support in England had been taken from her. She had lived the last two years with a relative who was now dead. "And he also is my cousin,—a distant cousin—you understand that."

"And do you love him?"

"Love him! What; as you loved her whom you have lost?—as she loved you when she clung to you before she went? No; certainly not. I shall never know anything of that love."

"And is he good?"

"He is a hard man. Men become hard when they deal in money as he has done. He was home five years since, and then I swore to myself that I would not marry him. But his letters to me are kind."

Forrest sat silent for a minute or two, for they were up in the bow again, seated on the sail that was bound round the bowsprit, and then he answered her, "A woman should never marry a man unless she loves him."

"Ah," says she, "of course you will condemn me. That is the way in which women are always treated. They have no choice given them, and are then scolded for choosing wrongly."

"But you might have refused him."

"No; I could not. I cannot make you understand the whole, —how it first came about that the marriage was proposed, and agreed to by me under certain conditions. Those conditions have come about, and I am now bound to him. I have taken his money and have no escape. It is easy to say that a woman should not marry without love, as easy as it is to say that a man should not starve. But there are men who starve,—starve although they work hard."

"I did not mean to judge you, Miss Viner."

"But I judge myself, and condemn myself so often. Where should I be in half an hour from this if I were to throw myself forward into the sea? I often long to do it. Don't you feel tempted sometimes to put an end to it all?"

"The waters look cool and sweet, but I own I am afraid of the bourne beyond."

"So am I, and that fear will keep me from it."

"We are bound to bear our burden of sorrow. Mine, I know, is heavy enough."

"Yours, Mr. Forrest! Have you not all the pleasures of memory to fall back on, and every hope for the future? What can I remember, or what can I hope? But, however, it is near eight o'clock, and they have all been at tea this hour past. What will my Cerberus say to me? I do not mind the male mouth, if only the two feminine mouths could be stopped." Then she rose and went back to the stern of the vessel; but as she slid into a seat, she saw that Mrs. Grumpy was standing over her.

From thence to St. Thomas the voyage went on in the customary manner. The sun became very powerful, and the passengers in the lower part of the ship complained loudly of having their portholes closed. The Spaniards sat gambling in the cabin all day, and the ladies prepared for the general move which was to be made at St. Thomas. The alliance between Forrest and Miss Viner went on much the same as ever, and Mrs. Grumpy said very ill-natured things. On one occasion she ventured to lecture Miss Viner; but that lady knew how to take her own part, and Mrs. Grumpy did not get the best of it. The dangerous alliance, I have said, went on the same as ever; but it must not be supposed that either person in any way committed aught that was wrong. They sat together and talked together, each now knowing the other's circumstances; but had it not been for the prudish caution of some of the ladies there would have been nothing amiss. As it was there was not much amiss. Few of the passengers really cared whether or no Miss Viner had found an admirer. Those who were going down to Panama were mostly Spaniards, and as the great separation became nearer, people had somewhat else of which to think.

And then the separation came. They rode into that pretty harbour of St. Thomas early in the morning, and were ignorant, the most of them, that they were lying in the very worst centre of yellow fever among all those plague-spotted islands. St. Thomas is very pretty as seen from the ships; and when that has been said, all has been said that can be said in its favour.[11] There was a busy, bustling time of it then. One vessel after another was brought up along side of the big ship that had come from England, and each took its separate freight of passengers and luggage. First started the boat that ran down the Leeward Islands to Demerara, taking with her Mr. Grumpy and all his family.

"Good-bye, Miss Viner," said Mrs. Grumpy. "I hope you'll get quite safely to the end of your voyage; but do take care."

"I'm sure I hope everything will be right," said Amelia, as she absolutely kissed her enemy. It is astonishing how well young women can hate each other, and yet kiss at parting.

"As to everything being right," said Miss Viner, "that is too much to hope. But I do not know that anything is going especially wrong.—Good-bye, Sir," and then she put out her hand to Mr. Grumpy. He was at the moment leaving the ship laden with umbrellas, sticks, and coats, and was forced to put them down in order to free his hand.

"Well, good-bye," he said. "I hope you'll do, till you meet your friends at the Isthmus."

"I hope I shall, sir," she replied; and so they parted.

Then the Jamaica packet started.

"I dare say we shall never see each other again," said Morris, as he shook his friend's hand heartily. "One never does. Don't interfere with the rights of that gentleman in Peru, or he might run a knife into you."

"I feel no inclination to injure him on that point."

"That's well; and now good-bye." And thus they also were parted. On the following morning the branch ship was dispatched to Mexico; and then, on the afternoon of the third day that for Colon—as we Englishmen call the town on this side of the Isthmus of Panama. Into that vessel Miss Viner and Mr. Forrest moved themselves and their effects; and now that the three-headed Cerberus was gone, she had no longer hesitated in allowing him to do for her all those little things which it is well that men should do for women when they are travelling. A woman without assistance under such circumstances is very forlorn, very apt to go to the wall, very ill able to assert her rights as to accommodation; and I think that few can blame Miss Viner for putting herself and her belongings under the care of the only person who was disposed to be kind to her.

Late in the evening the vessel steamed out of St. Thomas' harbour, and as she went Ralph Forrest and Emily Viner were standing together at the stern of the boat looking at the retreating lights of the Danish town. If there be a place on the earth's surface odious to me, it is that little Danish isle to which so many of our young seamen are sent to die,—there being no good cause whatever for such sending. But the question is one which cannot well be argued here.

"I have five more days of self and liberty left me," said Miss Viner. "That is my life's allowance."

"For heaven's sake do not say words that are so horrible."

"But am I to lie for heaven's sake, and say words that are false; or shall I be silent for heaven's sake, and say nothing during these last hours that are allowed to me for speaking? It is so. To you I can say that it is so, and why should you begrudge me the speech?"

"I would begrudge you nothing that I could do for you."

"No, you should not. Now that my incubus has gone to Barbadoes, let me be free for a day or two. What chance is there, I wonder, that the ship's machinery should all go wrong, and that we should be tossed about in the seas here for the next six months? I suppose it would be very wicked to wish it?"

"We should all be starved; that's all."

"What, with a cow on board, and a dozen live sheep, and thousands of cocks and hens! But we are to touch at Santa Martha and Cartagena. What would happen to me if I were to run away at Santa Martha?"

"I suppose I should be bound to run with you."

"Oh, of course. And therefore, as I would not wish to destroy you, I won't do it. But it would not hurt you much to be shipwrecked, and wait for the next packet."

"Miss Viner," he said after a pause,—and in the meantime he had drawn nearer to her, too near to her considering all things —"in the name of all that is good, and true, and womanly, go back to England. With your feelings, if I may judge of them by words which are spoken half in jest—"

"Mr. Forrest, there is no jest."

"With your feelings a poorhouse in England would be better than a palace in Peru."

"An English workhouse would be better, but an English poorhouse is not open to me. You do not know what it is to have friends—no, not friends, but people belonging to you— just so near as to make your respectability a matter of interest to them, but not so near that they should care for your happiness. Emily Viner married to Mr. Gorloch in Peru is put out of the way respectably. She will cause no further trouble, but her name may be mentioned in family circles without annoyance. The fact is, Mr. Forrest, that there are people who have no business to live at all."

"I would go back to England," he added, after another pause. "When you talk to me with such bitterness of five more days of living liberty you scare my very soul. Return, Miss Viner, and brave the worst. He is to meet you at Panama. Remain on this side of the Isthmus, and send him word that you must return. I will be the bearer of the message."

"And shall I walk back to England?" said Miss Viner.

"I had not quite forgotten all that," he replied, very gently. "There are moments when a man may venture to propose that which under ordinary circumstances would be a liberty.

Money, in a small moderate way, is not greatly an object to me. As a return for my valiant defence of you against your West Indian Cerberus, you shall allow me to arrange that with the agent at Colon."

"I do so love plain English, Mr. Forrest. You are proposing, I think, to give me something about fifty guineas."

"Well, call it so if you will," said he, "if you will have plain English that is what I mean."

"So that by my journey out here, I should rob and deceive the man I do know, and also rob the man I don't know. I am afraid of that bourne beyond the waters of which we spoke; but I would rather face that than act as you suggest."

"Of the feelings between him and you, I can of course be no judge."

"No, no; you cannot. But what a beast I am not to thank you! I do thank you. That which it would be mean in me to take, it is noble, very noble, in you to offer. It is a pleasure to me—I cannot tell why—but it is a pleasure to me to have had the offer. But think of me as a sister, and you will feel that it would not be accepted;—could not be accepted, I mean, even if I could bring myself to betray that other man."

Thus they ran across the Caribbean Sea, renewing very often such conversations as that just given. They touched at Santa Martha and Cartagena on the coast of the Spanish main, and at both places he went with her on shore. He found that she was fairly well educated, and anxious to see and to learn all that might be seen and learned in the course of her travels. On the last day, as they neared the Isthmus, she became more tranquil and quiet in the expression of her feelings than before, and spoke with less of gloom than she had done.

"After all ought I not to love him?" she said. "He is coming all the way up from Callao merely to meet me. What man would go from London to Moscow to pick up a wife?"

"I would—and thence round the world to Moscow again—if she were the wife I wanted."

"Yes; but a wife who has never said that she loved you! It is purely a matter of convenience. Well; I have locked my big box, and I shall give the key to him before it is ever again unlocked. He has a right to it, for he has paid for nearly all that it holds."

"You look at things from such a mundane point of view."

"A woman should, or she will always be getting into difficulty. Mind, I shall introduce you to him, and tell him all that you have done for me. How you braved Cerberus and the rest of it."

"I shall certainly be glad to meet him."

"But I shall not tell him of your offer;—not yet at least. If he be good and gentle with me, I shall tell him that too after a time. I am very bad at keeping secrets,—as no doubt you have perceived. We go across the Isthmus at once; do we not?"

"So the Captain says."

"Look!"—and she handed him back his own field-glass. "I can see the men on the wooden platform. Yes; and I can see the smoke of an engine." And then, in little more than an hour from that time the ship had swung round on her anchor.

Colon, or Aspinwall as it should be called, is a place in itself as detestable as St. Thomas.[12] It is not so odious to an Englishman, for it is not used by Englishmen more than is necessary. We have no great depot of traffic there, which we might with advantage move elsewhere. Taken, however, on its own merits, Aspinwall is not a detestable place. Luckily, however, travellers across the Isthmus to the Pacific are never doomed to remain there long. If they arrive early in the day, the railway thence to Panama takes them on at once. If it be not so, they remain on board ship till the next morning. Of course it will be understood that the transit line chiefly affects Americans, as it is the highroad from New York to California.

In less than an hour from their landing, their baggage had been examined by the Custom House officers of New Grenada, and they were on the railway cars, crossing the Isthmus. The officials in those out-of-the-way places always seem like apes imitating the doings of men. The officers at Aspinwall open and look at the trunks just as monkeys might do, having clearly no idea of any duty to be performed, nor any conception that goods of this or that class should not be allowed to pass. It is the thing in Europe to examine luggage going into a new country; and why should not they be as good as Europeans?

"I wonder whether he will be at the station?" she said, when the three hours of the journey had nearly passed. Forrest could perceive that her voice trembled as she spoke, and that she was becoming nervous.

"If he has already reached Panama, he will be there. As far as I could learn the arrival up from Peru had not been telegraphed."

"Then I have another day,—perhaps two. We cannot say how many. I wish he were there. Nothing is so intolerable as suspense."

"And the box must be opened again."

When they reached the station at Panama they found that the vessel from the South American coast was in the roads, but that the passengers were not yet on shore. Forrest, therefore, took Miss Viner down to the hotel, and there remained with her, sitting next to her in the common drawing-room of the house, when she had come back from her own bedroom. It would be necessary that they should remain there four or five days, and Forrest had been quick in securing a room for her. He had assisted in taking up her luggage, had helped her in placing her big box, and had thus been recognized by the crowd in the hotel as her friend. Then came the tidings that the passengers were landing, and he became nervous as she was. "I will go down and meet him," said he, "and tell him that you are here. I shall soon find him by his name." And so he went out.

Everybody knows the scrambling manner in which passengers arrive at an hotel out of a big ship. First came two or three energetic, heated men, who, by dint of screeching and bullying, have gotten themselves first disposed. They always get the worst rooms at the inns, the housekeepers having a notion that the richest people, those with the most luggage, must be more tardy in their movements. Four or five of this nature passed by Forrest in the hall, but he was not tempted to ask questions of them. One, from his age, might have been Mr. Gorloch, but he instantly declared himself to be Count Sapparello. Then came an elderly man alone, with a small bag in his hand. He was one of those who pride themselves on going from pole to pole without encumbrance, and who will be behoved to no one for the carriage of their luggage. To him, as he was alone in the street, Forrest addressed himself. "Gorloch," said he. "Gorloch: are you a friend of his?"

"A friend of mine is so," said Forrest.

"Ah, indeed; yes," said the other. And then he hesitated. "Sir," he then said, "Mr. Gorloch died at Callao, just seven days before the ship sailed. You had better see Mr. Cox." And then the elderly man passed in with his little bag.

Mr. Gorloch was dead. "Dead!" said Forrest, to himself, as he leaned back against the wall of the hotel still standing on the street pavement. "She has come out here; and now he is gone!" And then a thousand thoughts crowded on him. Who should tell her? And how would she bear it? Would it in truth be a relief to her to find that that liberty for which she had sighed had come to her? Or now that the testing of her feelings had come to her, would she regret the loss of home and wealth, and such position as life in Peru would give her? And above all would this sudden death of one who was to have been so near to her, strike her to the heart?

But what was he to do? How was he now to show his friendship? He was returning slowly in at the hotel door, where crowds of men and women were now thronging, when he was addressed by a middle-aged, good-looking gentleman, who asked him whether his name was Forrest. "I am told," said the gentleman, when Forrest had answered him, "that you are a friend of Miss Viner's. Have you heard the sad tidings from Callao?" It then appeared that this gentleman had been a stranger to Mr. Gorloch, but had undertaken to bring a letter up to Miss Viner. This letter was handed to Mr. Forrest, and he found himself burdened with the task of breaking the news to his poor friend. Whatever he did do, he must do at once, for all those who had come up by the Pacific steamer knew the story, and it was incumbent on him that Miss Viner should not hear the tidings in a sudden manner and from a stranger's mouth.

He went up into the drawing-room, and found Miss Viner seated there in the midst of a crew of women. He went up to her, and taking her hand, asked her in a whisper whether she would come out with him for a moment.

"Where is he?" said she. "I know that something is the matter. What is it?"

"There is such a crowd here. Step out for a moment." And he led her away to her own room.

"Where is he?" said she. "What is the matter? He has sent to say that he no longer wants me. Tell me; am I free from him?"

"Miss Viner, you are free."

Though she had asked the question herself, she was astounded by the answer; but, nevertheless, no idea of the truth had yet come upon her. "It is so," she said. "Well, what else? Has he written? He has bought me, as he would a beast of burden, and has, I suppose, a right to treat me as he pleases."

"I have a letter; but, dear Miss Viner—"

"Well, tell me all,—out at once. Tell me everything."

"You are free, Miss Viner; but you will be cut to the heart when you learn the meaning of your freedom."

"He has lost everything in trade. He is ruined."

"Miss Viner, he is dead!"

She stood staring at him for a moment or two, as though she could not realize the information which he gave her. Then gradually she retreated to the bed, and sat upon it. "Dead, Mr. Forrest!" she said. He did not answer her, but handed her the letter, which she took and read as though it were mechanically. The letter was from Mr. Gorloch's partner, and told her everything which it was necessary that she should know.

"Shall I leave you now?" he said, when he saw that she had finished reading it.

"Leave me; yes,—no. But you had better leave me, and let me think about it. Alas me, that I should have so spoken of him!"

"But you have said nothing unkind."

"Yes; much that was unkind. But spoken words cannot be recalled. Let me be alone now, but come to me soon. There is no one else here than I can speak to."

He went out, and finding that the hotel dinner was ready, he went in and dined. Then he strolled into the town, among the hot, narrow, dilapidated streets; and then, after two hours' absence, returned to Miss Viner's room. When he knocked, she came and opened the door, and he found that the floor was strewed with clothes. "I am preparing, you see, for my return. The vessel starts back for St. Thomas the day after to-morrow."

"You are quite right to go,—to go at once. Oh, Miss Viner! Emily, now at least you must let me help you."

He had been thinking of her most during those last two hours, and her voice had become pleasant to his ears, and her eyes very bright to his sight.

"You shall help me," she said. "Are you not helping me when at such a time you come to speak to me?"

"And you will let me think that I have a right to act as your protector?"

"My protector! I do know that I want such aid as that. During the days that we are here together you shall be my friend."

"You shall not return alone. My journeys are nothing to me. Emily, I will return with you to England."

Then she rose up from her seat and spoke to him.

"Not for the world," she said. "Putting out of question the folly of your forgetting your own objects, do you think it possible that I should go with you, now that he is dead? To you I have spoken of him harshly; and now that it is my duty to mourn for him, could I do so heartily if you were with me? While he lived, it seemed to me that in those last days I had a right to speak my thoughts plainly. You and I were to part and meet no more, and I regarded us both as people apart, who for a while might drop the common usages of the world. It is so no longer. Instead of going with you farther, I must ask you to forget that we were ever together."

"Emily, I shall never forget you."

"Let your tongue forget me. I have given you no cause to speak good of me, and you will be too kind to speak evil."

After that she explained to him all that the letter had contained. The arrangements for her journey had all been made; money also had been sent to her; and Mr. Gorloch in his will had provided for her, not liberally, seeing that he was rich, but still sufficiently.

And so they parted at Panama. She would not allow him even to cross the Isthmus with her, but pressed his hand warmly as he left her at the station. "God bless you!" he said. "And may God bless you, my friend!" she answered.

Thus alone she took her departure for England, and he went on his way to California.

Miss Ophelia Gledd

Who can say what is a lady? My intelligent and well-bred reader of either sex will at once declare that he and she knows very well who is a lady. So, I hope, do I. But the present question goes further than that. What is it, and whence does it come? Education does not give it, nor intelligence, nor birth, not even the highest. The thing, which in its presence or absence is so well known and understood, may be wanting to the most polished manners, to the sweetest disposition, to the truest heart. There are thousands among us who know it at a glance, and can recognise its presence from the sound of a dozen words, but there is not one among us who can tell us what it is.

Miss Ophelia Gledd was a young lady of Boston, Massachusetts, and I should be glad to know whether in the estimation of my countrymen and countrywomen she is to be esteemed a lady.

An Englishman, even of the best class, is often at a loss to judge of the "ladyship" of a foreigner, unless he has really lived in foreign cities and foreign society; but I do not know that he is ever so much puzzled in this matter by any nationality as he is by the American.

American women speak his own language, read his own literature, and in many respects think his own thoughts; but there have crept into American society so many little social ways at variance with our social ways, there have been wafted thither so many social atoms which there fit into their places, but which with us would clog the wheels, that the words, and habits, and social carriage, of an American woman, of the best class, too often offend the taste of an Englishman; as do, quite as strongly, those of the Englishwoman offend the American.

There are those who declare that there are no American ladies; but these are people who would probably declare the same of the French and the Italians, if the languages of France and Italy were as familiar to their ears as is the language of the States. They mean that American women do not grow up to be

English ladies,—not bethinking themselves that such a growth was hardly to be expected. Now I will tell my story, and ask my readers to answer this question,—Was Miss Ophelia Gledd a lady?

When I knew her she was at any rate great in the society of Boston, Massachusetts, in which city she had been as well known for the last four or five years as the yellow dome of the State House. She was as pure and perfect a specimen of a Yankee girl as ever it was my fortune to know.

Standing about five feet eight, she seemed to be very tall, because she always carried herself at her full height. She was thin too, and rather narrower at the shoulders than the strictest rules of symmetry would have made her. Her waist was very slight; so much so, that to the eye it would seem that some unjust and injurious force had created its slender compass; but I have fair ground for stating my belief that no such force had been employed. But yet, though she was slight and thin, and even narrow, there was a vivacity and quickness about all her movements, and an easiness in her mode of moving which made it impossible to deny to her the merit of a pleasing figure.

No man would, I think, at first sight, declare her to be pretty, and certainly no woman would do so; and yet I have seldom known a face in the close presence of which it was more gratifying to sit, and talk, and listen. Her brown hair was always brushed close off from her forehead. Her brow was high, and her face narrow and thin; but that face was ever bright with motion, and her clear, deep, grey eyes, full of life and light, were always ready for some combat or some enterprise. Her nose and mouth were the best features in her face, and her teeth were perfect,—miracles of perfection; but her lips were too thin for feminine beauty; and indeed such personal charms as she had were not the charms which men love most,— sweet changing colour, soft full flowing lines of grace, and womanly gentleness in every movement. Ophelia Gledd had none of these. She was hard and sharp in shape, of a good brown steady colour, hard and sharp also in her gait; with no full flowing lines, with no softness; but she was bright as burnished steel.

And yet she was the belle of Boston. I do not know that any man of Boston,—or any stranger knowing Boston would have ever declared that she was the prettiest girl in the city; but this was certain almost to all,—that she received more of that admiration which is generally given to beauty than did any other lady there; and that the upper social world of Boston had become so used to her appearance, such as it was, that no one ever seemed to question the fact of her being a beauty. She had been passed as a beauty by examiners whose certificate in that matter was held to be good, and had received high rank as a beauty in the drawing-rooms at Boston.

The fact was never questioned now, unless by some passing stranger who would be told in flat terms that he was wrong.

"Yes, sir; you'll find you're wrong; you'll find you aire, if you'll bide here awhile."

I did bide there awhile, and did find that I was wrong. Before I left I was prepared to allow that Miss Ophelia Gledd was a beauty. And moreover, which was more singular, all the women allowed it.

Ophelia Gledd, though the belle of Boston, was not hated by the other belles. The female feeling with regard to her was, I think this, that the time had arrived in which she should choose her husband, and settle down, so as to leave room for others less attractive than herself.

When I knew her she was very fond of men's society; but I doubt if any one could fairly say that Miss Gledd ever flirted. In the proper sense of the word she certainly never flirted. Interesting conversations with interesting young men at which none but themselves were present she had by the dozen. It was as common for her to walk up and down Beacon Street,—the parade of Boston,—with young Jones, or Smith, or more probably with young Mr. Optimus M. Opie, or young Mr. Hannibal H. Hoskins, as it is for our young Joneses, and young Smiths, and young Hoskinses, to saunter out together.

That is the way of the country, and no one took wider advantage of the ways of her own country than did Miss Ophelia Gledd. She told young men also when to call upon her, if she liked them; and in seeking or in avoiding their society, did very much as she pleased.

But these practices are right or wrong, not in accordance with a fixed rule of morality prevailing over all the earth,—such a rule, for instance, as that which orders men not to steal; but they are right or wrong according to the usages of the country in which they are practised.

In Boston it is right that Miss Ophelia Gledd should walk up Beacon Street with Hannibal Hoskins the morning after she has met him at a ball, and that she should invite him to call upon her at twelve o'clock on the following day.

She had certainly a nasal twang in speaking. Before my intercourse with her was over, her voice had become pleasant in my ears, and it may be that that nasal twang which had at first been so detestable to me, had recommended itself to my sense of hearing. At different periods of my life I have learned to love an Irish brogue and a northern burr.

Be that as it may, I must acknowledge that Miss Ophelia Gledd spoke with a certain nasal twang. But then such is the manner of speech at Boston; and she only did that which the Joneses and Smiths, the Opies and Hoskinses, were doing around her.

Ophelia Gledd's mother was, for a living being, the nearest thing to a nonentity that I ever met. Whether within her own house in Chesnut Street she exerted herself in her domestic duties and held authority over her maidens I cannot say, but neither in her dining parlour nor in her drawing-room did she hold any authority. Indeed, throughout the house, Ophelia was paramount, and it seemed as though her mother could not venture on a hint in opposition to her daughter's behests.

Mrs. Gledd never went out, but her daughter frequented all balls, dinners, and assemblies, which she chose to honour. To all these she went alone, and had done since she was eighteen years of age. She went also to lectures, to meetings of wise men, for which the Western Athens is much noted, to political debates, and wherever her enterprising heart and inquiring head chose to carry her. But her mother never went anywhere; and it always seemed to me that Mrs. Gledd's intercourse with her domestics must have been nearer, closer, and almost dearer to her, than any that she could have with her daughter.

Mr. Gledd had been a merchant all his life. When Ophelia Gledd first came before the Boston world he had been a rich merchant; and as she was an only child she had opened her campaign with all the advantages which attach to an heiress. But now, in these days, Mr. Gledd was known to be a merchant without riches. He still kept the same house, and lived apparently as he had always lived; but the world knew that he had been a broken merchant and was now again struggling. That Miss Gledd felt the disadvantage of this no one can, I suppose, doubt. But she never showed that she felt it. She spoke openly of her father's poverty as of a thing that was known, and of her own. Where she had been exigeant before, she was exigeant now. Those she disliked when rich she disliked now that she was poor. Where she had been patronising before, she patronised now. Where she had loved, she still loved. In former days she had a carriage, and now she had none. Where she had worn silk, she now wore cotton. In her gloves, her laces, her little belongings there was all the difference which money makes or the want of money; but in her manner there was none.

Nor was there any difference in the manner of others to her. The loss of wealth seemed to entail on Miss Gledd no other discomfort than the actual want of those things which hard money buys. To go in a coach might have been a luxury to her, and that she had lost; but she had lost none of her ascendancy, none of her position, none of her sovereignty.

I remember well where, when, and how, I first met Miss Gledd. At that time her father's fortune was probably already gone, but if so, she did not then know that it was gone.

It was in winter,—towards the end of winter,—when the passion for sleighing became ecstatic. I expect all my readers to know that sleighing is the grand winter amusement of Boston. And indeed it is not bad fun. There is the fashionable course for sleighing,—the Brighton Road, and along that you drive, seated among furs, with a young lady beside you if you can get one to trust you; your horse or horses carry little bells, which add to the charms; the motion is rapid and pleasant, and, which is the great thing, you see and are seen by everybody. Of course it is expedient that the frost should be sound and perfect, so that the sleigh should run over a dry, smooth surface. But as the season draws to an end, and when sleighing intimacies have become close and warm, the horses are made to travel through slush and wet, and the scene becomes one of peril and discomfort, though one also of excitement, and not unfrequently of love.

Sleighing was fairly over at the time of which I now speak, so that the Brighton Road was deserted in its slush and sloppiness. Nevertheless, there was a possibility of sleighing; and as I was a stranger newly arrived, a young friend of mine, took me, or rather allowed me to take him out, so that the glory of the charioteer might be mine.

"I guess we're not alone," said he, after we had passed the bridge out of the town. "There's young Hoskins and Pheely Gledd just a-head of us."[13]

That was the first I had ever heard of Ophelia, and then as I pushed along after her, instigated by a foolish Briton's ambition to pass the Yankee whip, I did hear a good deal about her; and in addition to what has already been told, I then heard that this Mr. Hannibal Hoskins, to pass whom on the road was now my only earthly desire, was Miss Gledd's professed admirer; in point of fact, that it was known to all Boston that he had offered his hand to her more than once already.

"She has accepted him now, at any rate," said I, looking at their close contiguity on the sleigh before me. But my friend explained to me that such was by no means probable; that Miss Gledd had twenty hangers-on of the same description, with any one of whom she might be seen sleighing, walking, or dancing; but that no argument as to any further purpose on her part was to be deduced from any such practice. "Our girls," said my friend, "don't go about tied to their mothers' aprons, as girls do in the old country. Our free institutions," &c., &c. I confessed my blunder, and acknowledged that a wide and perhaps salutary latitude was allowed to the feminine creation on his side of the Atlantic. But, do what I would, I couldn't pass Hannibal Hoskins. Whether he guessed that I was an ambitious Englishman, or whether he had a general dislike to be passed on the road, I don't know; but he raised his whip to his horses and went away from us suddenly and very quickly through the slush. The snow was half gone, and hard ridges of it remained across the road, so that his sleigh was bumped about most uncomfortably. I soon saw that his horses were running away, and that Hannibal Hoskins was in a fix. He was standing up, pulling at them with all his strength and weight, and the carriage was yawing about and across the road in a manner that made us fear it would go to pieces. Miss Ophelia Gledd, however, kept her seat, and there was no shrieking. In about five minutes they were well planted into a ditch, and we were alongside of them.

"You fixed that pretty straight, Hoskins," said my friend.

"Darn them for horses," said Hoskins, as he wiped the perspiration from his brow and looked down upon the fiercest of the quadrupeds, sprawling up to his withers in the snow. Then he turned to Miss Gledd, who was endeavouring to unroll herself from her furs.

"Oh, Miss Gledd, I am so sorry. What am I to say?"

"You'd better say that the horses ran away, I think," said Miss Gledd. Then she stepped carefully out, on to a buffalo-robe, and moved across from that, quite dry-footed, on to our sleigh. As my friend and Hoskins were very intimate, and could, as I thought, get on very well by themselves with the debris in the ditch, I offered to drive Miss Gledd back to town. She looked at me with eyes which gave me, as I thought, no peculiar thanks, and then remarked that she had come out with Mr. Hoskins, and that she would go back with him.

"Oh, don't mind me," said Hoskins, who was at that time up to his middle in snow.

"Ah, but I do mind you," said Ophelia. "Don't you think we could go back and send some people to help these gentlemen?"

It was the coolest proposition that I had ever heard, but in two minutes Miss Gledd was putting it into execution. Hannibal Hoskins was driving her back in the sledge which I had hired, and I was left with my friend to extricate those other two brutes from the ditch.

"That's so like Pheely Gledd," said my friend. "She always has her own way."

Then it was that I questioned Miss Gledd's beauty, and was told that before long I should find myself to be wrong. I had almost acknowledged myself to be wrong before that night was over.

I was at a tea-party that same evening at which Miss Gledd was present;—it was called a tea-party though I saw no tea. I did, however, see a large hot supper, and a very large assortment of long-necked bottles. I was standing rather listlessly near the door, being short of acquaintance, when a young Yankee dandy, with a very stiff neck, informed me that Miss Gledd wanted to speak to me. Having given me this intimation he took himself off with an air of disgust, among the long-necked bottles.

"Mr. Green," she said,—I had just been introduced to her as she was being whisked away by Hoskins in my sleigh—"Mr. Green, I believe I owe you an apology. When I took your sleigh from you I didn't know you were a Britisher,—I didn't, indeed."[14]

I was a little nettled, and endeavoured to explain to her that an Englishman would be just as ready to give up his carriage to a lady as any American.

"Oh, dear, yes; of course," she said. "I didn't mean that; and now I've put my foot into it worse than ever; I thought you were at home here, and knew our ways, and if so you wouldn't mind being left with a broken sleigh."

I told her that I didn't mind it. That what I had minded was the being robbed of the privilege of driving her home, which I had thought to be justly mine.

"Yes," said she, "and I was to leave my friend in the ditch! That's what I never do. You didn't suffer any disgrace by remaining there till the men came."

"I didn't remain there till any men came. I got it out and drove it home."

"What a wonderful man! But then you're English. However, you can understand that if I had left my driver he would have been disgraced. If ever I go out anywhere with you, Mr.

Green, I'll come home with you. At any rate it shan't be my fault if I don't." After that I couldn't be angry with her, and so we became great friends.

Shortly afterwards the crash came; but Miss Gledd seemed to disregard the crash altogether, and held her own in Boston. As far as I could see there were just as many men desirous of marrying her as ever, and among the number Hannibal H. Hoskins was certainly no defaulter.

My acquaintance with Boston had become intimate; but, after a while, I went away for twelve months, and when I returned, Miss Gledd was still Miss Gledd. "And what of Hoskins?" I said to my friend,—the same friend who had been with me in the sleighing expedition.

"He's just on the old tack. I believe he proposes once a-year regularly. But they say now that she's going to marry an Englishman."

It was not long before I had an opportunity of renewing my friendship with Miss Gledd,—for our acquaintance had latterly amounted to a friendship,—and of seeing the Englishman with her. As it happened, he also was a friend of my own,—an old friend, and the last man in the world whom I should have picked out as a husband for Ophelia. He was a literary man of some mark, fifteen years her senior, very sedate in his habits, not much given to love-making, and possessed of a small fortune sufficient for his own wants, but not sufficient to enable him to marry with what he would consider comfort. Such was Mr. Pryor, and I was given to understand that Mr. Pryor was a suppliant at the feet of Ophelia. He was a suppliant, too, with so much hope, that Hannibal Hoskins and the other suitors were up in arms against him. I saw them together at some evening assembly, and on the next morning I chanced to be in Miss Gledd's drawing-room. On my entrance there were others there, but the first moment that we were alone, she turned round sharp upon me with a question,—

"You know your countryman, Mr. Pryor; what sort of a man is he?"

"But you know him also," I answered. "If the rumours in Boston are true, he is already a favourite in Chesnut Street."

"Well, then, for once in a way the rumours in Boston are true, for he is a favourite. But that is no reason you shouldn't tell me what sort of a man his is. You've known him these ten years."

"Pretty nearly twenty," I said,—I had known him ten or twelve.

"Ah," said she, "you want to make him out to be older than he is. I knew his age today."

"And does he know yours?"

"He may if he wishes it. Everybody in Boston knows it,— including yourself. Now tell me; what sort of man is Mr. Pryor?"

"He is a man highly esteemed in his own country."

"So much I knew before; and he is highly esteemed here also. But I hardly understand what high estimation means in your country."

"It is much the same thing in all countries, as I take it," said I.

"There you are absolutely wrong. Here in the States, if a man be highly esteemed it amounts almost to everything; such estimation will carry him everywhere,—and will carry his wife everywhere too, so as to give her a chance of making standing ground for herself."

"But Mr. Pryor has not got a wife."

"Don't be stupid. Of course he hasn't got a wife, and of course you know what I mean."

But I did not know what she meant. I knew that she was meditating whether or no it would be good for her to become Mrs. Pryor, and that she was endeavouring to get from me some information which might assist her in coming to a decision on that matter; but I did not understand the exact gist and point of her inquiry.

"You have so many prejudices of which we know nothing," she continued. "Now don't put your back up and fight for that blessed old country of yours, as though I were attacking it."

"It is a blessed old country," said I, patriotically.

"Quite so; very blessed, and very old,—and very nice too, I'm sure. But you must admit that you have prejudices. You are very much the better, perhaps, for having them. I often wish that we had a few." Then she stopped her tongue, and asked no further question about Mr. Pryor; but it seemed to me that she wanted me to go on with the conversation.

"I hate discussing the relative merits of the two countries," said I; "and I especially hate to discuss them with you. You always begin as though you meant to be fair, and end by an amount of unfairness, that—that——"

"Which would be insolent if I were not a woman, and which is pert as I am one. That is what you mean."

"Something like it."

"And yet I love your country so dearly, that I would sooner live there than in any other land in the world, if only I thought that I could be accepted. You English people," she continued, "are certainly wanting in intelligence, or you would read in the anxiety of all we say about England how much we all think of you. What will England say of us? what will England think of us? what will England do in this or that matter as it concerns us? that is our first thought as to every matter that is of importance to us. We abuse you, and admire you. You abuse us, and despise us. That is the difference. So you won't tell me anything about Mr. Pryor? Well, I shan't ask you again. I never again ask a favour that has been refused." Then she turned away to some old gentleman that was talking to her mother, and the conversion was at an end.

I must confess, that as I walked away from Chesnut Street into Beacon Street, and across the Common, my anxiety was more keen with regard to Mr. Pryor than as concerned Miss Gledd. He was an Englishman and an old friend, and being also a man not much younger than myself, he was one regarding whom I might, perhaps, form some correct judgment as to what would and what would not suit him. Would he do well in taking Ophelia Gledd home to England with him as his wife? Would she be accepted there, as she herself had phrased it,— accepted in such fashion as to make him contented? She was intelligent,—so intelligent that few women whom she would meet in her proposed new country could beat her there; she was pleasant, good-humoured, true, as I believed; but would she be accepted in London? There was a freedom and easiness about her, a readiness to say anything that came into her mind, an absence of all reticence, which would go very hard with her in London. But I never had heard her say anything that she should not have said. Perhaps, after all, we have got our prejudices in England. When next I met Pryor, I spoke to him about Miss Gledd.

"The long and the short of it is," I said; "that people say that you are going to marry her."

"What sort of people?"

"They were backing you against Hannibal Hoskins the other night at the club, and it seemed clear that you were the favourite."

"The vulgarity of these people surpasses anything that I ever dreamed of," said Pryor. "That is, of some of them. It's all very well for you to talk, but could such a bet as that be proposed in the open room of any club in London?"

"The clubs in London are too big, but I dare say it might down in the country. It would be just the thing for Little Pedlington."

"But Boston is not Little Pedlington. Boston assumes to be the Athens of the States. I shall go home by the first boat next month." He had said nothing to me about Miss Gledd, but it was clear that if he went home by the first boat next month, he would go home without a wife; and as I certainly thought that the suggested marriage was undesirable, I said nothing to persuade him to remain at Boston.

It was again sleighing time, and some few days after my meeting with Pryor I was out upon the Brighton Road in the thick of the crowd. Presently I saw the hat and back of Hannibal Hoskins, and by his side was Ophelia Gledd. Now, it must be understood that Hannibal Hoskins, though he was in many respects most unlike an English gentleman, was neither a fool nor a bad fellow. A fool he certainly was not. He had read much. He could speak glibly, as is the case with all Americans. He was scientific, classical, and poetical,—probably not to any great depth. And he knew how to earn a large income with the full approbation of his fellow-citizens. I had always hated him since the day on which he had driven Miss Gledd home; but I had generally attributed my hatred to the manner in which he wore his hat on one side. I confess I had often felt amazed that Miss Gledd should have so far encouraged him. I think I may at any rate declare that he would not have been accepted in London,—not accepted for much! And yet Hannibal Hoskins was not a bad fellow. His true devotion to Ophelia Gledd proved that.

"Miss Gledd," said I, speaking to her from my sleigh, "do you remember your calamity? There is the very ditch not a hundred yards ahead of you."

"And here is the very knight that took me home in your sleigh," said she, laughing.

Hoskins sat bolt upright and took off his hat. Why he took off his hat I don't know, unless that thereby he got an opportunity of putting it on again a little more on one side.

"Mr. Hoskins would not have the goodness to upset you again, I suppose?" said I.

"No, sir," said Hoskins; and he raised the reins and squared up his elbows, meaning to look like a knowing charioteer. "I guess we'll go back; eh, Miss Gledd?"

"I guess we will," said she. "But, Mr. Green, don't you remember that I once told you if you'd take me out, I'd be sure to come home with you? You never tried me, and I take it bad of you." So encouraged I made an engagement with her, and in two or three days' time from that I had her beside me in my sleigh on the same road.

By this time I had quite become a convert to the general opinion, and was ready to confess in any presence, that Miss Gledd was a beauty. As I started with her out of the city warmly enveloped in buffalo furs, I could not but think how nice it would be to drive on and on, so that nobody should ever catch us. There was a sense of companionship about her in which no woman that I have ever known excelled her. She had a way of adapting herself to the friend of the moment which was beyond anything winning. Her voice was decidedly very pleasant; and as to that nasal twang I am not sure that I was ever right about it. I wasn't in love with her myself, and didn't want to fall in love with her. But I felt that I should have liked to cross the Rocky Mountains with her, over to the Pacific, and to have come home round by California, Peru, and the Pampas. And for such a journey I should not at all have desired to hamper the party with the society either of Hannibal Hoskins or of Mr. Pryor! "I hope you feel that you're having your revenge," said she.

"But I don't mean to upset you."

"I almost wish you would, so as to make it even. And my poor friend Mr. Hoskins would feel himself so satisfied. He says you Englishmen are conceited about your driving."

"No doubt, he thinks we are conceited about everything."

"So you are, and so you should be. Poor Hannibal! He is wild with despair because ———"

"Because what?"

"Oh, never mind. He is an excellent fellow, but I know you hate him."

"Indeed, I don't."

"Yes, you do; and so does Mr. Pryor. But he is so good! You can't either understand or appreciate the kind of goodness which our young men have. Because he pulls his hat about, and can't wear his gloves without looking stiff, you won't remember that out of his hard earnings he gives his mother and sisters everything that they want."

"I didn't know anything of his mother and sisters."

"No, of course you didn't. But you know a great deal about his hat and gloves. You are too hard, and polished, and well-mannered in England to know anything about anybody's mother or sisters, or indeed to know anything about anybody's anything. It is nothing to you whether a man be moral, or affectionate, or industrious, or good-tempered. As long as he can wear his hat properly, and speak as though nothing on the earth, or over the earth, or under the earth, could ever move him, that is sufficient."

"And yet I thought you were so fond of England?"

"So I am. I too like,—nay, love that ease of manner which you all possess and which I cannot reach."

Then there was silence between us for perhaps half a mile,

and yet I was driving slow, as I did not wish to bring our journey to an end. I had fully made up my mind that it would be in every way better for my friend Pryor that he should give up all thoughts of his Western Aspasia, and yet I was anxious to talk to her about him as though such a marriage were still on the cards.[15] It had seemed that lately she had thrown herself much into an intimacy with myself, and that she was anxious to speak openly to me if I would only allow it. But she had already declared, on a former occasion, that she would ask me no further question about Mr. Pryor. At last I plucked up courage, and put to her a direct proposition about the future tenour of her life. "After all that you have said about Mr. Hoskins, I suppose I may expect to hear that you have at last accepted him?" I could not have asked such a question of any English girl that I ever knew,—not even of my own sister in these plain terms. And yet she took it not only without anger, but even without surprise. And she answered it, as though I had asked her the most ordinary question in the world.

"I wish I had," she said. "That is, I think I wish I had. It is certainly what I ought to do."

"Then why do you not do it?"

"Ah! why do I not? Why do we not all do just what we ought to do? But why am I to be cross-questioned by you? You would not answer me a question when I asked you the other day."

"You tell me that you wish you had accepted Mr. Hoskins. Why do you not do so?" said I, continuing my cross-examination.

"Because I have a vain ambition,—a foolish ambition,—a silly, moth-like ambition,—by which, if I indulge it, I shall only burn my wings. Because I am such an utter ass that I would fain make myself an Englishwoman."

"I don't see that you need burn your wings!"

"Yes; should I go there I shall find myself to be nobody, whereas here I am in good repute. Here I could make my husband a man of mark by dint of my own power. There I doubt whether even his esteen would so shield and cover me as to make me endurable. Do you think that I do not know the difference; that I am not aware of what makes social excellence there? And yet, though I know it all, and covet it, I despise it. Social distinction with us is given on sounder terms than it is with you, and is more frequently the deserved reward of merit. Tell me; if I go to London they will ask who was my grandfather?"

"Indeed, no; they will not ask even of your father unless you speak of him."

"No; their manners are too good. But they will speak of their fathers, and how shall I talk with them? Not but what my grandfather was a good man; and you are not to suppose that I am ashamed of him because he stood in a store and sold leather with his own hands. Or rather I am ashamed of it. I should tell my husband's old friends and my new acquaintances that it was so because I am not a coward; and yet as I told them I should be ashamed. His brother is what you call a baronet."

"Just so!"

"And what would the baronet's wife say to me with all my sharp Boston notions? Can't you see her looking at me over the length of the drawing-room? And can't you fancy how pert I should be, and what snappish words I should say to the she baronet? Upon the whole, don't you think I should do better with Mr. Hoskins?"

Again I sat silent for some time. She had now asked me a question to which I was bound to give her a true answer,—an answer that should be true as to herself without reference to Pryor. She was sitting back in the sleigh, tamed as it were by her own thoughts, and she had looked at me as though she had really wanted counsel. "If I am to answer you in truth—" I said.

"You are to answer me in truth."

"Then," said I, "I can only bid you take him of the two whom you love; that is, if it be the case that you love either."

"Love!" she said.

"And if it be the case," I continued, "that you love neither, then leave them both as they are."

"I am not then to think of the man's happiness?"

"Certainly not by marrying him without affection."

"Ah! but I may regret him,—with affection."

"And for which of them do you feel affection?" I asked. And as I asked, we were already within the streets of Boston.

She again remained silent, almost till I had placed her at her own door; then she looked at me with eyes full, not only of meaning, but of love also;—with that in her eyes for which I had not hitherto given her credit.

"You know the two men," she said, "and do you ask me that?" When these words were spoken, she jumped from the sleigh, and hurried up the steps to her father's door. In very truth, the hat and gloves of Hannibal Hoskins had influenced her as they had influenced me, and they had done so although she knew how devoted he was as a son and a brother.

For a full month after that I had no further conversation with Miss Gledd or with Mr. Pryor on the subject. At this time I was living in habits of daily intimacy with Pryor, but as he did not speak to me about Ophelia, I did not often mention her name to him. I was aware that he was often with her,—or at any rate often in her company. But I did not believe that he had any daily habit of going to the house, as he would have done had he been her accepted suitor. And indeed I believed him to be a man who would be very persevering in offering his love; but who, if persistently refused, would not probably tender it again. He still talked of returning to England, though he had fixed no day. I myself purposed doing so early in May, and used such influence as I had in endeavouring to keep him at Boston till that time. Miss Gledd, also, I constantly saw. Indeed, one could not live in the society of Boston without seeing her almost daily, and I was aware that Mr. Hoskins was frequently with her. But, as regarded her, this betokened nothing, as I have before endeavoured to explain. She never deserted a friend, and had no idea of being reserved in her manners with a man because it was reported that such man was her lover. She would be very gracious to Hannibal in Mr. Pryor's presence; and yet it was evident, at any rate to me, that in doing so, she had no thought of grieving her English admirer.

I was one day seated in my room at the hotel when a servant brought me up a card. "Misther Hoskins; he's a waiting below, and wants to see yer honour very partickler," said the raw Irishman. Mr. Hoskins had never done me the honour of calling on me before, nor had I ever become intimate with him even at the club; but, nevertheless, as he had come to me, of course I was willing to see him, and so he was shown up into my room. When he entered, his hat was, I suppose, in his hand; but it looked as though it had been on one side of his head the moment before, and as though it would be on one side again the moment he left me.

"I beg your pardon, Mr. Green," said he. "Perhaps I ought not to intrude upon you here."

"No intrusion at all. Won't you take a chair, and put your hat down?" He did take a chair, but he wouldn't put his hat down. I confess that I had been actuated by a foolish desire to see it placed for a few minutes in a properly perpendicular position.

"I've just come,—I'll tell you why I've come. There are some things, Mr. Green, in which a man doesn't like to be interfered with." I could not but agree with this, but in doing so I expressed a hope that Mr. Hoskins had not been interfered with to any very disagreeable extent. "Well!" I scorn to say that the Boston dandy said "wa'all," but if this story were written by any Englishman less conscientious than myself, that latter form of letters is the one which he would adopt in his endeavour to convey the sound as uttered by Mr. Hoskins. "Well, I don't quite know about that. Now, Mr. Green, I'm not a quarrelsome man. I don't go about with six-shooters in my pocket, and I don't want to fight, nohow, if I can help it."

In answer to this I was obliged to tell him that I sincerely hoped that he would not have to fight; but that if fighting became necessary to him, I trusted that his fighting propensities would not be directed against any friend of mine.

"We don't do much in that way on our side of the water," said I.

"I am well aware of that," said he. "I don't want any one to teach me what are usages of genteel life in England. I was there the whole fall, two years ago."

"As regards myself," said I, "I don't think much good was ever done by duelling."[16]

"That depends, sir, on how things eventuate. But, Mr. Green, satisfaction of that description is not what I desiderate on the present occasion. I wish to know whether Mr. Pryor is, or is not, engaged to marry Miss Ophelia Gledd."

"If he is, Mr. Hoskins, I don't know it."

"But, sir, you are his friend."

This I admitted, but again assured Mr. Hoskins that I knew nothing of any such engagement. He pleaded also that I was her friend as well as his. This, too, I admitted, but again declared that from neither side had I been made aware of the fact of any such engagement.

"Then, Mr. Green," said he, "may I ask you for your own private opinion?"

Upon the whole I was inclined to think that he might not, and so I told him in what most courteous words I could find for the occasion. His bust at first grew very long and stiff, and his hat became more and still more sloped as he held it. I began to fear that, though he might not have a six-shooter in his pocket, he had nevertheless some kind of pistol in his thoughts. At last he started up on his feet and confronted me, as I thought, with a look of great anger. But his words when they came were no longer angry.

"Mr. Green," said he, "if you knew all that I've done to get that girl!"

My heart was instantly softened to him.

"For aught that I know," said I, "you may have her this moment for asking."

"No," said he, "no." His voice was very melancholy, and as he spoke he looked into his sloping hat. "No; I've just come from Chesnut Street, and I think she's rather more turned against me than ever."

He was a tall man, good-looking after a fashion, dark, with thick black shiny hair, and huge bold moustachioes. I myself do not like his style of appearance, but he certainly had a manly bearing. And in the society of Boston generally he was regarded as a stout fellow, well able to hold his own; as a man, by no means soft, or green, or feminine. And yet now, in the presence of me, a stranger to him, he was almost crying about his lady love. In England no man tells another that he has been rejected; but then in England so few men tell to others anything of their real feeling. As Ophelia had said to me, we are hard and polished, and nobody knows anything about anybody's anything. What could I say to him? I did say something. I went so far as to assure him that I had heard Miss Gledd speak of him in the highest language; and at last perhaps I hinted,—though I don't think I did quite hint it,—that if Pryor were out of the way, Hoskins might find the lady more kind. He soon became quite confidential, as though I were his bosom friend. He perceived, I think, that I was not anxious that Pryor should carry off the prize, and he wished me to teach Pryor that the prize was not such a prize as would suit him.

"She's the very girl for Boston," he said, in his energy; "but, I put it to you, Mr. Green, she hasn't the gait of going that would suit London."

Whether her gait of going would or would not suit our metropolis, I did not undertake to say in the presence of Mr. Hoskins, but I did at last say that I would speak to Pryor, so that the field might be left open for others if he had no intention of running for the cup himself.

I could not but be taken, and indeed charmed, by the honest strength of affection which Hannibal Hoskins felt for the object of his adoration. He had come into my room determined to display himself as a man of will, of courage, and of fashion. But he had broken down in all that, under his extreme desire to obtain assistance in getting the one thing which he wanted. When he parted with me he shook hands almost boisterously, while he offered me most exuberant thanks. And yet I had not suggested that I could do anything for him. I did think that Ophelia Gledd would accept his offer as soon as Pryor was gone; but I had not told him that I thought so.

About two days afterwards I had a very long and a very serious conversation with Pryor, and at that time I do not think that he had made up his mind as to what he intended to do. He was the very opposite to Hoskins in all his ways and all his moods. There was not only no swagger with him, but a propriety and quiescence of demeanour the very opposite to swagger. In conversation his most violent opposition was conveyed by a smile. He displayed no other energy than what might be shown in the slight curl of his upper lip. If he reproved you he did it by silence. There could be no greater contrast than that between him and Hoskins, and there could be no doubt which man would recommend himself most to our English world by his gait and demeanour. But I think there may be a doubt as to which was the best man, and a doubt also as to which would make the best husband. That my friend was not then engaged to Miss Gledd I did learn,—but I learned nothing further,—except this, that he would take his departure with me the first week in May, unless anything special occurred to keep him in Boston.

It was some time early in April that I got a note from Miss Gledd, asking me to call on her.

"Come at once," she said, "as I want your advice above all things." And she signed herself, "Yours in all truth, O. G."

I had had many notes from her, but none written in this strain; and therefore, feeling that there was some circumstance to justify such instant notice, I got up and went to her then, at ten o'clock in the morning. She jumped up to meet me, giving me both her hands.

"Oh, Mr. Green," she said to me, "I am so glad you have come to me. It is all over."

"What is over?" said I.

"My chance of escape from the she baronet. I gave in last night. Pray tell me that I was right. Yet I want you to tell me the truth. And yet, above all things, you must not tell me that I have been wrong."

"Then you have accepted Mr. Pryor?"

"I could not help it," she said. "The temptation was too much for me. I love the very cut of his coat, the turn of his lip, the tone of his voice. The very sound which he makes as he closes the door behind him is too much for me. I believe that I ought to have let him go,—but I could not do it."

"And what will Mr. Hoskins do?"

"I wrote to him immediately and told him everything. Of course I had John's leave for doing so."

This calling of my sedate friend by the name of John was, to my feeling, a most wonderful breaking down of all proprieties.

"I told him the exact truth. This morning I got an answer from him saying that he should visit Russia. I am so sorry because of his mother and sisters."

"And when is it to be?"

"Oh, at once, immediately. So John says. When we resolve on doing these things here, on taking the plunge, we never stand shilly-shallying on the brink as your girls do in England. And that is one reason why I have sent for you. You must promise to go over with us. Do you know I am half afraid of him,—much more afraid of him than I am of you."

They were to be married very early in May, and of course I promised to put off my return for a week or two to suit them.

"And then for the she baronet," she said, "and for all the terrible grandeur of London!"

When I endeavoured to explain to her that she would encounter no great grandeur, she very quickly corrected me.

"It is not grandeur of that sort, but the grandeur of coldness that I mean. I fear that I shall not do for them. But, Mr. Green, I must tell you one thing. I have not cut off from myself all means of retreat."

"Why, what do you mean? You have resolved to marry him."

"Yes, I have promised to do so; but I did not promise till he had said that if I could not be made to suit his people in Old England, he would return here with me and teach himself to suit my people in New England. The task will be very much easier."

They were married in Boston, not without some considerable splendour of ceremony,—as far as the splendour of Boston went. She was so unusual a favourite that every one wished to be at her wedding, and she had no idea of giving herself airs and denying her friends a favour. She was married with much *éclat*, and, as far as I could judge, seemed to enjoy the marriage herself.

Now comes the question; will she or will she not be received in London as a lady,—as such a lady as my friend Pryor might have been expected to take for his wife?

Charles Dickens

It seems to have been but the other day that, sitting where I now sit, in the same chair, at the same table, with the same familiar things around me, I wrote for the "Cornhill Magazine" a few lines in remembrance of Thackeray, who had then been taken from us; and, when those lines appeared, they were preceded by others, very full of feeling, from his much older friend, Charles Dickens. Now I take up my pen again, because Charles Dickens has also gone, and because it is not fit that this publication should go forth without a word spoken to his honour.[17]

It is singular that two men in age so nearly equal, in career so nearly allied, friends so old, and rivals so close, should each have left us so suddenly, without any of that notice, first doubting and then assured, which illness gives;—so that in the case of the one as of the other, the tidings of death's dealings have struck us a hard and startling blow, inflicting, not only sorrow, but for a while that positive, physical pain which comes from evil tidings which are totally unexpected. It was but a week or two since that I was discussing at the club that vexed question of American copyright with Mr. Dickens, and, while differing from him somewhat, was wondering at the youthful vitality of the man who seemed to have done his forty years of work without having a trace of it left upon him to lessen his energy, or rob his feelings of their freshness. It was but the other day that he spoke at the Academy dinner, and those who heard him then heard him at his best; and those who did not hear him, but only read his words, felt how fortunate it was that there should be such a man to speak for literature on such an occasion.[18] When he took farewell of the public as a public reader, a few months since, the public wondered that a man in the very prime of his capacity should retire from such a career. But though there was to be an end of his readings, there was not, therefore, to be an end of his labours. He was to resume, and did resume, his old work, and when the first number of Edwin Drood's Mystery was bought up with unprecedented avidity by the lovers of Dickens's stories, it was feared, probably, by none but one that he might not live to finish his chronicle. He was a man, as we all thought, to live to be a hundred. He looked to be full of health, he walked vigorously, he stood, and spoke, and, above all, he laughed like a man in the full vigour of his life. He had never become impassive as men do who have grown old beneath burdens too heavy for their shoulders. Whatever he did seemed to come from him easily, as though he delighted in the doing of it. To hear him speak was to long to be a speaker oneself; because the thing, when properly managed, could evidently be done so easily, so pleasantly, with such gratification not only to all hearers but to oneself! We were, indeed, told some time since that he was ill, and must seek rest for awhile; but any one may be ill for a period. What working man does not suffer occasionally? But he never looked ill when he was seen at his work. As I am now writing, it is just two years and two months since I entered the harbour of New York as he was leaving it, and I then called on him on board the "Russia." I found him with one of his feet bound up, and he told me, with that pleasant smile that was so common to him, that he had lectured himself off his legs; otherwise he was quite well. When I heard afterwards of his labours in the States, and of the condition in which those labours had been continued, it seemed to be marvellous that any constitution should have stood it. He himself knew, no doubt, where the shoe pinched him, where the burden was too heavy, where the strain told,—that strain, without which such work as his could not adequately be done; but there was a vitality in the man, and a certain manliness of demeanour, which made those who looked upon him believe that nothing that he had yet done had acted injuriously upon the machine of his body. But that it had so acted there can now be but little doubt. We have been told that he complained in his own home that his present work was burdensome to him, and that the task of composition was difficult. When making pecuniary arrangements for the publication of "Edwin Drood" he especially stipulated by deed that the publishers should be reimbursed for any possible loss that might accrue to them should he be prevented by death or sickness from completing his work,—a stipulation which can hardly have been necessary, but which, as it betrays his own nervousness, so also gives evidence of his high honour and thoughtful integrity.

The event, which he alone thought probable enough to require provision, has taken place; and "Edwin Drood," like "Denis Duval," and "Wives and Daughters,"—the novel on which Mrs. Gaskell was engaged when she died,—will be left unfinished.[19] To speak here of the circumstances of his life,—or of the manner of the sad catastrophe which has taken him from us,—would be unnecessary. The daily and weekly newspapers have already told the public all that can be told at once;—and that which will require later and careful telling, will we hope be told with care. Of the man's public work and public character it may perhaps not be amiss for one who remembers well the "Sketches by Boz" when they first came out, to say a few words. Of his novels, the first striking circumstance is their unprecedented popularity. This is not the time for exact criticism; but, even were it so, no critic is justified in putting aside the consideration of that circumstance. When the masses of English readers, in all English-reading countries, have agreed to love the writings of any writer, their verdict will be stronger than that of any one judge, let that judge be ever so learned and ever so thoughtful. However the writer may have achieved his object, he has accomplished that which must be the desire of every author,—he has spoken to men and women who have opened their ears to his words, and have listened to them. He has reached the goal which all authors seek. In this respect Dickens was, probably, more fortunate during his own life than any writer that ever lived. The English-speaking public may be counted, perhaps, as a hundred millions, and wherever English is read these books are popular from the highest to the lowest,—among all classes that read. In England his novels are found in every house in which books are kept; but in America his circulation is much more extended than it is in England, because the houses in which books exist are much more numerous. I remember another novelist saying to me of Dickens,—my friend and his friend, Charles Lever,[20]—that

Dickens knew exactly how to tap the ever newly-growing mass of readers as it sprang up among the lower classes. He could measure the reading public,—probably taking his measure of it unconsciously,—and know what the public wanted of him. Consequently the sale of his books has been hitherto so far from ephemeral,—their circulation has been so different from that which is expected for ordinary novels,—that it has resembled in its nature the sales of legs of mutton or of loaves of bread. The butcher or baker will know how many of this or of that article he will "do" in a summer or in a winter quarter, and so does the bookseller know how many "Pickwicks" and how many "Nicklebys" he will "do." That there should be an average and continued demand for books as for other commodities, is not astonishing. That readers should require an increasing number of Shakespeares, or of Euclids, or of "Robinson Crusoes," is not strange. But it is very strange that such a demand of an author's works should have grown up during his own life, that the demand should be made in regard to novels, that it should have continued with unabated force,—and that it should exceed, as I believe it does exceed, the demand for the works of any other one writer in the language.

And no other writer of English language except Shakespeare has left so many types of character as Dickens has done,—characters which are known by their names familiarly as household words, and which bring to our minds vividly and at once, a certain well-understood set of ideas, habits, phrases, and costumes, making together a man, or woman, or child, whom we know at a glance and recognise at a sound,—as we do our own intimate friends. And it may be doubted whether even Shakespeare has done this for so wide a circle of acquaintances. To constant readers of Shakespeare, Iago and Shylock, Rosalind and Juliet, Falstaff and Sir Toby, Lear and Lady Macbeth, have their characters so clearly discernible as to have become a part and parcel of their lives;—but such readers are as yet comparatively few in numbers. And other great authors have achieved the same thing with, perhaps, one or two characters. Bobadil, Squire Western, the Vicar of Wakefield, and Colonel Newcomb, are among out very intimate friends and have become types.[21] With Scott's characters, glorious as they are, this is hardly the case. We know well the characters, as Scott has drawn them, of Ivanhoe, Meg Merrilies, Mr. Oldbuck, Balfour of Burley, and the Master of Ravenswood;—but we know them as creations of Scott, and not as people in our own every-day world. We never meet with Meg Merrilies, or have any among our acquaintance whom we rank as being of the order of Ivanhoe. If we saw them in the flesh we should not recognise them at a glance. But Pickwick and Sam Weller, Mrs. Nickleby and Wackford Squeers, Fagin and Bill Sikes, Micawber, Mrs. Gamp, Pecksniff, and Bucket the Detective, are persons so well known to us that we think that they, who are in any way of the professions of these worthies, are untrue to themselves if they depart in aught from their recognised and understood portraits. Pickwick can never be repeated;—nulli similis aut secundus, he is among our dearest and nearest, and we expect no one to be like him. But a "boots" at an hotel is more of a boots the closer he resembles Sam Weller. Many ladies talk like Mrs. Nickleby, and are perfect or imperfect in our estimation as they adhere or depart from their great prototype. With murderous Jews and their murdering agents we have probably but a distant acquaintance, but we fancy that they should be as are Fagin and Sikes. A schoolmaster who lives by starving his boys will certainly have but one eye, as was the case with Mr. Squeers. The man with whom something is ever about to turn up, is well-known to us, and is always considered by us to be going under an alias when he is not called Micawber. The lady who follows a certain profession that has ever been open to ladies is no longer called by the old name, but is Mrs. Gamp. Every hypocrite who knows his part, wears the Pecksniff shirt-collar. Every detective is to us a Bucket. And Dickens has given us conventional phrases of which everybody knows the meaning, though many are ignorant whence they come. To have "one's greens on one's mind" is as good English as "to be at sea" or "to be down in the mouth;" but many who can do nothing while their greens are on their mind, who are always talking of their greens, forget that the phrase began with that old warrior Mrs. Bagnet.

Most of us have probably heard Dickens's works often criticised, want of art in the choice of words and want of nature in the creation of character, having been the faults most frequently attributed to him. But his words have been so potent, whether they may be right or wrong according to any fixed rule, that they have justified themselves by making themselves into a language which is in itself popular; and his characters, if unnatural, have made a second nature by their own force. It is fatuous to condemn that as deficient in art which has been so full of art as to captivate all men. If the thing be done which was the aim of the artist,—fully done,—done beyond the power of other artists to accomplish,—the time for criticising the mode of doing it is gone by. Rules are needed in order that a certain effect may be obtained;—but if the effect has certainly been obtained, what need to seek whether or no the rule has been obeyed? The example, indeed, may be dangerous to others; as they have found who have imitated Dickens, and others will find who may imitate him in future.

It always seemed to me that no man ever devoted himself so entirely as Charles Dickens to things which he understood, and in which he could work with effect. Of other matters he seemed to have a disregard,—and for many things almost a contempt which was marvellous. To literature in all its branches his attachment was deep,—and his belief in it was a thorough conviction. He could speak about it as no other man spoke. He was always enthusiastic in its interests, ready to push on beginners, quick to encourage those who were winning their way to success, sympathetic with his contemporaries, and greatly generous to aid those who were failing. He thoroughly believed in literature; but in politics he seemed to have no belief at all. Men in so-called public life were to him, I will not say insincere men, but so placed as to be by their calling almost beyond the pale of sincerity. To his feelings, all departmental work was the bungled, muddled routine of a Circumlocution Office.[22] State-craft was odious to him; and though he would probably never have asserted that a country could be maintained without legislative or executive, he seemed to regard such devices as things so prone to evil, that

the less of them the better it would be for the country,—and
the further a man kept himself from their immediate influence
the better it would be for him. I never heard any man call
Dickens a radical; but if any man ever was so, he was a radical
at heart,—believing entirely in the people, writing for them,
speaking for them, and always desirous to take their part as
against some undescribed and indiscernible tyrant, who to his
mind loomed large as an official rather than as an aristocratic
despot. He hardly thought that our parliamentary rulers could
be trusted to accomplish ought that was good for us. Good
would come gradually,—but it would come by the strength of
the people, and in opposition to the blundering of our rulers.

No man ever kept himself more aloof than Dickens from the
ordinary honours of life. No titles were written after his name.
He was not C.B., or D.C.L., or F.R.S.; nor did he ever
attempt to become M.P. What titles of honour may ever have
been offered to him, I cannot say; but that titles were offered I
do not doubt. Lord Russell, a year or two ago, proposed a
measure by which, if carried, certain men of high character and
great capacity would have been selected as peers for life; but
Charles Dickens would never have been made a lord.[23] He
probably fully appreciated his own position; and had a noble
confidence in himself, which made him feel that nothing
Queen, Parliament, or Minister, could do for him would make
him greater than he was. No title to his ear could have been
higher than that name which he made familiar to the ears of all
reading men and women.

He would attempt nothing,—show no interest in anything,
—which he could not do, and which he did not understand.
But he was not on that account forced to confine himself to
literature. Every one knows how he read. Most readers of these
lines, though they may never have seen him act,—as I never
did,—still know that his acting was excellent. As an actor he
would have been at the top of his profession. And he had
another gift,—had it so wonderfully, that it may almost be said
that he has left no equal behind him. He spoke so well, that a
public dinner became a blessing instead of a curse, if he was in
the chair,—had its compensating twenty minutes of pleasure,

even if he were called upon to propose a toast, or to thank the company for drinking his health. For myself, I never could tell how far his speeches were ordinarily prepared;—but I can declare that I have heard him speak admirably when he has had to do so with no moment of preparation.

A great man has gone from us;—such a one that we may surely say of him that we shall not look upon his like again. As years roll on, we shall learn to appreciate his loss. He now rests in the spot consecrated to the memory of our greatest and noblest; and Englishmen would certainly not have been contented had he been laid elsewhere.

A Walk in a Wood

The most difficult thing that a man has to do is to think. There are many who can never bring themselves really to think at all, but do whatever thinking is done by them in a chance fashion, with no effort, using the faculty which the Lord has given them because they cannot, as it were, help themselves. To think is essential, all will agree. That it is difficult most will acknowledge who have tried it. If it can be compassed so as to become pleasant, brisk, and exciting as well as salutary, much will have been accomplished. My purpose here is to describe how this operation, always so difficult, often so repugnant to us, becomes easier out among the woods, with the birds and the air and the leaves and the branches around us, than in the seclusion of any closet.

But I have nothing to show for it beyond my own experience, and no performances of thought to boast of beyond the construction of combinations in fiction, countless and unimportant as the sand on the sea-shore. For in these operations of thinking it is not often the entire plot of a novel,—the plot of a novel as a whole,—that exercises the mind. That is a huge difficulty;—one so arduous as to have been generally found by me altogether beyond my power of accomplishment. Efforts are made no doubt,—always out in the open air, and within the precincts of a wood if a wood be within reach; but to construct a plot so as to know, before the story is begun, how it is to end, has always been to me a labour of Hercules beyond my reach. I have to confess that my incidents are fabricated to fit my story as it goes on, and not my story to fit my incidents. I wrote a novel once in which a lady forged a will; but I had not myself decided that she had forged it till the chapter before that in which she confesses her guilt. In another a lady is made to steal her own diamonds,—a grand tour-de-force, as I thought, —but the brilliant idea only struck me when I was writing the page in which the theft is described. I once heard an unknown critic abuse my workmanship because a certain lady had been made to appear too frequently in my pages. I went home and killed her immediately.[24] I say this to show that the process of thinking to which I am alluding has not generally been applied to any great effort of construction. It has expended itself on the minute ramifications of tale-telling;—how this young lady should be made to behave herself with that young gentleman; —how this mother or that father would be affected by the ill conduct or the good of a son or a daughter;—how these words or those other would be most appropriate and true to nature if used on some special occasion. Such plottings as these, with a fabricator of fiction, are infinite in number as they are infinitesimal in importance,—and are therefore, as I have said, like the sand of the sea-shore. But not one of them can be done fitly without thinking. My little effort will miss its wished-for result, unless I be true to nature; and to be true to nature I must think what nature would produce. Where shall I go to find my thoughts with the greatest ease and most perfect freedom?

Bad noises, bad air, bad smells, bad light, an inconvenient attitude, ugly surroundings, little misfortunes that have lately been endured, little misfortunes that are soon to come, hunger and thirst, overeating and overdrinking, want of sleep or too much of it, a tight boot, a starched collar, are all inimical to thinking. I do not name bodily ailments. The feeling of heroism which is created by the magnanimity of overcoming great evils will sometimes make thinking easy. It is not the sorrows but the annoyances of life which impede. Were I told that the bank had broken in which my little all was kept for me I could sit down and write my love story with almost a sublimated vision of love; but to discover that I had given half a sovereign instead of sixpence to a cabman would render a great effort necessary before I could find the fitting words for a lover. These little lacerations of the spirit, not the deep wounds, make the difficulty. Of all the nuisances named noises are the worst. I know a hero who can write his leading article for a newspaper in a club smoking-room while all the chaff of all the Joneses and all the Smiths is sounding in his ears;—but he is a hero because he can do it. To think with a barrel organ within hearing is heroic. For myself I own that a brass band altogether incapacitates me. No sooner does the first note of the opening burst reach my ear than I start up, fling down my pen, and cast my thoughts disregarded into the abyss of some chaos which is always there ready to receive them. Ah, how terrible, often how vain, is the work of fishing, to get them out again! Here, in our quiet square, the beneficent police have done wonders for our tranquillity,[25]—not, however, without creating for me personally a separate trouble in having to encounter the stern reproaches of the middle-aged leader of the band when he asks me in mingled German and English accents whether I do not think that he too as well as I,—he with all his comrades, and then he points to the nine stalwart, well-cropped, silent and sorrowing Teutons around him,—whether he and they should not be allowed to earn their bread as well as I. I cannot argue the matter with him. I cannot make him understand that in earning my own bread I am a nuisance to no one. I can only assure him that I am resolute, being anxious to avoid the gloom which was cast over the declining years of one old philosopher. I do feel, however, that this comparative peace within the heart of a huge city is purchased at the cost of many tears. When, as I walk-abroad, I see in some small crowded street the ill-shod feet of little children spinning round in the perfect rhythm of a dance, two little tots each holding the other by their ragged duds while an Italian boy grinds at his big box, each footfall true to its time, I say to myself that a novelist's schemes, or even a philosopher's figures, may be purchased too dearly by the silencing of the music of the poor.

Whither shall a man take himself to avoid these evils, so that he may do his thinking in peace,—in silence if it may be possible? And yet it is not silence that is altogether necessary. The wood-cutter's axe never stopped a man's thought, nor the wind through the branches, nor the flowing of water, nor the singing of birds, nor the distant tingling of a chapel bell. Even the roaring of the sea and the loud splashing of the waves among the rocks do not impede the mind. No sounds coming from water have the effect of harassing. But yet the sea-shore has its disadvantages. The sun overhead is hot or the wind is strong,—or the very heaviness of the sand creates labour and distraction. A high road is ugly, dusty, and too near akin to the business of the world. You may calculate your five per cents. and your six per cents. with precision as you tramp along a high road. They have a weight of material interest which rises above dust. But if your mind flies beyond this;—if it attempts to deal with humour, pathos, irony, or scorn, you should take it away from the well-constructed walks of life. I have always found it impossible to utilise railroads for delicate thinking. A great philosopher once cautioned me against reading in railway carriages. "Sit still," said he, "and label your thoughts." But he was a man who had stayed much at home himself. Other men's thoughts I can digest when I am carried along at the rate of thirty miles an hour; but not my own.

Any carriage is an indifferent vehicle for thinking, even though the cushions be plump, and the road gracious,—not rough nor dusty,—and the horses going at their ease. There is a feeling attached to the carriage that it is there for a special purpose,—as though to carry one to a fixed destination; and that purpose, hidden perhaps but still inherent, clogs the mind. The end is coming, and the sooner it is reached the better. So at any rate thinks the driver. If you have been born to a carriage, and carried about listlessly from your childhood upwards, then, perhaps, you may use it for free mental exercise; but you must have been coaching it from your babyhood to make it thus effective.

On horseback something may be done. You may construct your villain or your buffoon as you are going across country. All the noise of an assize court or the low rattle of a gambling table may thus be arranged. Standing by the covert side I myself have made a dozen little plots, and were I to go back to the tales I could describe each point at the covert side at which the incident or the character was moulded and brought into shape. But this, too, is only good for rough work. Solitude is necessary for the task we have in hand; and the bobbing up and down of the horse's head is antagonistic to solitude.

I have found that I can best command my thoughts on foot, and can do so with the most perfect mastery when wandering through a wood. To be alone is of course essential. Companionship requires conversation,—for which indeed the spot is most fit; but conversation is not now the object in view. I have found it best even to reject the society of a dog, who, if he be a dog of manners, will make some attempt at talking.[26] And though he should be silent the sight of him provokes words and caresses and sport. It is best to be away from cottages, away from children, away as far as may be from other chance wanderers. So much easier is it to speak than to think that any slightest temptation suffices to carry away the idler from the harder to the lighter work. An old woman with a bundle of sticks becomes an agreeable companion, or a little girl picking wild fruit. Even when quite alone, when all the surroundings seem to be fitted for thought, the thinker will still find a difficulty in thinking. It is not that the mind is inactive, but that it will run exactly whither it is not bidden to go. With subtle ingenuity it will find for itself little easy tasks instead of settling itself down on that which it is its duty to do at once. With me, I own, it is so weak as to fly back to things already done,—which require no more thinking, which are perhaps unworthy of a place even in the memory,—and to revel in the ease of contemplating that which has been accomplished rather than to struggle for further performance. My eyes which should become moist with the troubles of the embryo heroine, shed tears as they call to mind the early sorrow of Mr. ——, who was married and made happy many years ago. Then,—when it comes to this,—a great effort becomes necessary, or that day will for him have no results. It is so easy to lose an hour in maundering over the past, and to waste the good things which have been provided in remembering instead of creating!

But a word about the nature of the wood! It is not always easy to find a wood, and sometimes when you have got it, it is but a muddy, plashy, rough-hewn congregation of ill-grown trees,—a thicket rather than a wood,—in which even contemplation is difficult and thinking is out of the question. He who has devoted himself to wandering in woods will know at the first glance whether the place will suit his purpose. A crowded undergrowth of hazel, thorn, birch, and alder, with merely a track through it, will by no means serve the occasion. The trees around you should be big and noble. There should be grass at your feet. There should be space for the felled or fallen princes of the forest. A roadway, with the sign of wheels that have passed long since, will be an advantage, so long as the branches above head shall meet or seem to meet each other. I will not say that the ground should not be level, lest by creating difficulties I shall seem to show that the fitting spot may be too difficult to be found; but, no doubt, it will be an assistance in the work to be done if occasionally you can look down on the tops of the trees as you descend, and again look up to them as with increasing height they rise high above your head. And it should be a wood,—perhaps a forest,—rather than a skirting of timber. You should feel that, if not lost, you are lose-able. To have trees around you is not enough unless you have many. You must have a feeling as of Adam in the garden. There must be a confirmed assurance in your mind that you have got out of the conventional into the natural,—which will not establish itself unless there be a consciousness of distance between you and the next ploughed field. If possible you should not know the East from the West, or, if so, only by the setting of the sun. You should recognise the direction in which you must return simply by the fall of water.

But where shall the wood be found? Such woodlands there are still in England, though, alas, they are becoming rarer every year. Profit from the timber-merchant or dealer in firewood is looked to, or else, as is more probable, drives are cut broad and straight, like spokes of a wheel radiating to a nave or centre, good only for the purposes of the slayer of multitudinous pheasants. I will not say that a wood prepared, not as the home but the slaughter-ground of game, is altogether inefficient for our purpose. I have used such even when the sound of the guns has been near enough to warn me to turn my steps to the right or to the left. The scents are pleasant even in winter, the trees are there, and sometimes even yet the delightful feeling may be encountered that the track on which you are walking leads to some far off vague destination, in reaching which there may be much of delight because it will be new,—something also of peril because it will be distant. But the wood if possible should

seem to be purposeless. It should have no evident consciousness of being their either for game or fagots. The felled trunk
on which you sit should seem to have been selected for some
accidental purpose of house-building, as though a neighbour
had searched for what was wanting and had found it. No idea
should be engendered that it was let out at so much an acre to a
contractor who would cut the trees in order and sell them in the
next market. The mind should conceive that this wood never
had been planted by hands, but had come there from the direct
beneficence of the Creator,—as the first woods did come,—
before man had been taught to recreate them systematically,
and as some still remain to us, so much more lovely in their
wildness than when reduced to rows and quincunces, and
made to accommodate themselves to laws of economy and
order.

England, dear England,—and certainly with England Scotland also,—has advanced almost too far for this. There are still
woods, but they are so divided, and marked, and known, so
apportioned out among gamekeepers, park rangers, and other
custodians, that there is but little left of wildness in them. It is
too probable that the stray wanderer may be asked his purpose;
and if so, how will it be with him if he shall answer to the
custodian that he has come thither only for the purpose of
thinking? "But it's here my lord turns out his young pheasants!" "Not a feather from the wing of one of them shall be the
worse for me," answers the thinker. "I dun-na know," says the
civil custodian; "but it's here my lord turns out his young
pheasants." It is then explained that the stile into the field is but
a few yards off,—for our woodland distances are seldom very
great,—and the thinker knows that he must go and think
elsewhere. Then his work for that day will be over with him.
There are woods, however, which may with more or less
of difficulty be utilised. In Cumberland and Westmoreland
strangers are so rife that you will hardly be admitted beyond
the paths recognised for tourists. You may succeed on the sly,
and if so the sense of danger adds something to the intensity of
your thought. In Northamptonshire, where John the planter
lived, there are miles of woodland,—but they consist of

avenues rather than of trees. Here you are admitted and may trespass, but still with a feeling that game is the lord of all. In Norfolk, Suffolk, and Essex the gamekeepers will meet you at every turn,—or rather at every angle, for turns there are none. The woods have been all re-fashioned with measuring rod and tape. Two lines crossing each other, making what they call in Essex a four-want way, has no special offence, though if they be quite rectangular they tell something too plainly of human regularity; but four lines thus converging and radiating, displaying the brazen-faced ingenuity of an artificer, are altogether destructive of fancy. In Devonshire there are still some sweet woodland nooks, shaws, and holts, and pleasant spinneys, through which clear water brooks run, and the birds sing sweetly, and the primroses bloom early, and the red earth pressing up here and there gives a glow of colour,—and the gamekeeper does not seem quite as yet to dominate everything. Here, perhaps, in all fair England the solitary thinker may have his fairest welcome.

But though England be dear, there are other countries not so small, not so crowded, in which every inch of space has not been made so available either for profit or for pleasure, in which the woodland rambler may have a better chance of solitude amidst the unarranged things of nature. They who have written and they who have read about Australia say little and hear little as to its charm of landscape, but here the primeval forests running for uninterrupted miles, with undulating land and broken timber, with ways open everywhere through the leafy wilderness, where loneliness is certain till it be interrupted by the kangaroo, and where the silence is only broken by the noises of quaint birds high above your head, offer all that is wanted by him whose business it is to build his castles carefully in the air. Here he may roam at will and be interrupted by no fence, feel no limits, be wounded by no art, and have no sense of aught around him but the forest, the air, and the ground. Here too he may lose himself in truth till he shall think it well if he come upon a track leading to a shepherd's hut.

But the woods of Australia, New Zealand, California, or

South Africa are too far afield for the thinker for whom I am
writing. If he is to take himself out of England it must be
somewhere among the forests of Europe. France has still her
woodlands;—though for these let him go somewhat far afield,
nor trust himself to the bosky dells through which Parisian
taste will show him the way by innumerable finger posts. In the
Pyrenees he may satisfy himself, or on the sides of Jura. The
chesnut groves of Lucca, and the oak woods of Tuscany are
delightful where the autumnal leaves of Vallombrosa lie thick,
—only let him not trust himself to the mid-day sun. In Bel-
gium, as far as I know it, the woods are of recent growth, and
smack of profitable production. But in Switzerland there are
pure forests still, standing or appearing to stand as nature
caused them to grow, and here the poet or the novelist may
wander and find all as he would have it. Or, better still, let him
seek the dark shadows of the Black Forest, and there wander,
fancy free,—if that indeed can be freedom which demands a
bondage of its own.

Were I to choose the world all round I should take certain
districts in the Duchy of Baden as the hunting ground for my
thoughts. The reader will probably know of the Black Forest
that it is not continual wood. Nor, indeed, are the masses of
timber, generally growing on the mountain sides, or high
among the broad valleys, or on the upland plateaux, very large.
They are interspersed by pleasant meadows and occasional
cornfields, so that the wanderer does not wander on among
them, as he does, perhaps hopelessly, in Australia. But as the
pastures are interspersed through the forest, so is the forest
through the pastures; and when you shall have come to the
limit of this wood, it is only to be lured on into the confines of
the next. You go upwards among the ashes and beeches, and
oaks, till you reach the towering pines. Oaks have the pride of
magnificence; the smooth beech with its nuts thick upon it is a
tree laden with tenderness; the sober ash has a savour of
solitude, and of truth; the birch with its may-day finery
springing thick about it boasts the brightest green which nature
has produced; the elm,—the useless elm,—savours of decorum
and propriety; but for sentiment, for feeling, for grandeur, and

for awe, give me the forest of pines. It is when they are round me that, if ever, I can use my mind aright and bring it to the work which is required of it. There is a scent from them which reaches my brain and soothes it. There is a murmur among their branches, best heard when the moving breath of heaven just stirs the air, which reminds me of my duty without disturbing me. The crinkling fibres of their blossom are pleasant to my feet as I walk over them. And the colours which they produce are at the same time sombre and lovely, never paining the eye and never exciting it. If I can find myself here of an afternoon when there shall be another two hours for me, safe before the sun shall set, with my stick in my hand, and my story half-conceived in my mind, with some blotch of a character or two, just daubed out roughly on the canvas, then if ever I can go to work, and decide how he and she, and they shall do their work.

They will not come at once, those thoughts which are so anxiously expected,—and in the process of coming they are apt to be troublesome, full of tricks, and almost traitorous. They must be imprisoned, or bound with thongs, when they come, as was Proteus when Ulysses caught him amidst his sea-calves, —as was done with some of the fairies of old, who would, indeed, do their beneficent work, but only under compulsion. It may be that your spirit should on an occasion be as obedient as Ariel, but that will not be often. He will run backwards,—as it were downhill,—because it is so easy, instead of upward and onward. He will turn to the right and to the left, making a show of doing fine work, only not the work that is demanded of him that day. He will skip hither and thither, with pleasant bright gambols, but will not put his shoulder to the wheel, his neck to the collar, his hand to the plough. Has my reader ever driven a pig to market? The pig will travel on freely, but will always take the wrong turning, and then when stopped for the tenth time, will head backwards, and try to run between your legs. So it is with the tricksy Ariel,—that Ariel which every man owns, though so many of us fail to use him for much purpose, which but few of us have subjected to such discipline as Prospero had used before he had brought his servant to do his bidding at the slightest word.

It is right that a servant should do his master's bidding; and, with judicious discipline, he will do it. The great thinkers, no doubt, are they who have made their servant perfect in obedience, and quick at a moment's notice for all work. To them no adjuncts of circumstances are necessary. Solitude, silence, and beauty of surroundings are unnecessary. Such a one can bid his mind go work, and the task shall be done, whether in town or country, whether amid green fields, or congregated books or crowded assemblies. Such a master no doubt was Prospero. Such were Homer, and Cicero, and Dante. Such were Bacon and Shakespeare. They had so tamed, and trained, and taught their Ariels that each, at a moment's notice, would put a girdle round the earth. With us, though the attendant Spirit will come at last and do something at our bidding, it is but driving an unwilling pig to market.

But at last I feel that I have him,—perhaps by the tail, as the Irishman drives his pig. When I have got him I have to be careful that he shall not escape me till that job of work be done. Gradually as I walk, or stop, as I seat myself on a bank, or lean against a tree, perhaps as I hurry on waving my stick above my head till with my quick motion the sweat-drops come out upon my brow, the scene forms itself for me. I see, or fancy that I see, what will be fitting, what will be true, how far virtue may be made to go without walking upon stilts, what wickedness may do without breaking the link which binds it to humanity, how low ignorance may grovel, how high knowledge may soar, what the writer may teach without repelling by severity, how he may amuse without descending to buffoonery; and then the limits of pathos are searched, and words are weighed which shall suit, but do no more than suit, the greatness or the smallness of the occasion. We, who are slight, may not attempt lofty things, or make ridiculous with our little fables the doings of the gods. But for that which we do there are appropriate terms and boundaries which may be reached but not surpassed. All this has to be thought of and decided upon in reference to those little plotlings of which I have spoken, each of which has to be made the receptacle of pathos or of humour, of honour or of truth, as far as the thinker may be able to furnish them. He has to see, above all things, that in his attempts he shall not sin against nature, that in striving to touch the feelings he shall not excite ridicule, that in seeking for humour he does not miss his point, that in quest of honour and truth he does not become bombastic and straight-laced. A clergyman in his pulpit may advocate an altitude of virtue fitted to a millennium here or to a heaven hereafter;—nay, from the nature of his profession, he must do so. The poet too may soar as high as he will, and if words suffice to him, need never fear to fail because his ideas are too lofty. But he who tells tales in prose can hardly hope to be effective as a teacher unless he binds himself by the circumstances of the world which he finds around him. Honour and truth there should be, and pathos and humour, but he should so constrain them that they shall not seem to mount into nature beyond the ordinary habitations of men and women.

Such rules as to construction have probably been long known to him. It is not for them he is seeking as he is roaming listlessly or walking rapidly through the trees. They have come to him from much observation, from the writings of others, from that which we call study,—in which imagination has but little immediate concern. It is the fitting of the rules to the characters which he has created, the filling in with living touches and true colours those daubs and blotches on his canvas which have been easily scribbled with a rough hand, that the true work consists. It is here that he requires that his fancy should be undisturbed; that the trees should overshadow him, that the birds should comfort him, that the green and yellow mosses should be in unison with him,—that the very air should be good to him. The rules are there fixed,—fixed as far as his judgment can fix them, and are no longer a difficulty to him. The first coarse outlines of his story he has found to be a matter almost indifferent to him. It is with these little plotlings that he has to contend. It is for them that he must catch his Ariel, and bind him fast;—but yet so bind him that not a thread shall touch the easy action of his wings. Every little scene must be arranged so that,—if it may be possible,—the proper words may be spoken and the fitting effect produced.

Alas, with all these struggles, when the wood has been

found, when all external things are propitious, when the very heavens have lent their aid, it is so often that it is impossible! It is not only that your Ariel is untrained, but that the special Ariel which you may chance to own is no better than a rustic Hobgoblin, or a Peaseblossom, or Mustard Seed at the best. You cannot get the pace of the race-horse from a farm-yard colt, train him as you will. How often is one prompted to fling one's self down in despair, and, weeping between the branches, to declare that it is not that the thoughts will wander, it is not that the mind is treacherous. That which it can do it will do;—but the pace required from it should be fitted only for the farm-yard.

Nevertheless, before all be given up, let a walk in a wood be tried.

BIBLIOGRAPHICAL NOTE

"Malachi's Cove" first appeared in *Good Words*, December, 1864 and was reprinted in Trollope's third volume of short stories, *Lotta Schmidt and Other Stories*, 1867.

"Father Giles of Ballymoy" first appeared in *The Argossy*, May, 1866 and was reprinted in *Lotta Schmidt*.

"La Mère Bauche" was written for *Harper's New Monthly Magazine* in New York but not published there. Trollope included it in his first volume of short stories, *Tales of All Countries* (First Series), 1861.

"The Journey to Panama" was first published in Emily Faithfull's *Victoria Regia* (1861), edited by Adelaide Proctor. It was reprinted in *Lotta Schmidt*.

"Miss Ophelia Gledd" was first published in Emily Faithfull's *A Welcome: Original Contributions in Poetry and Prose*, 1863, and was reprinted in *Lotta Schmidt*.

"Charles Dickens" appeared in *St Paul's Magazine*, July, 1870.

"A Walk in a Wood" appeared in *Good Words*, September, 1879.

NOTES

Malachi's Cove

Page 1. 1. Trollope frequently uses "since" in its older meaning of "before".

Father Giles of Ballymoy

22. 2. Trollope was sent to Ireland in September, 1841. The potato crop failed four years later and led to the disastrous famine. For Trollope's comments on the famine see his novel, *Castle Richmond*, published in 1860. "Green" is a name Trollope frequently uses for the narrator in his short stories.

23. 3. Charles Bianconi was an Italian who set up a system of transportation throughout Ireland. According to Trollope's first biographer, T. H. S. Escott, Bianconi proved a great help to Trollope in devising shorter routes for his journeys. (Escott, *Anthony Trollope* (1913), pp. 44–5.) Trollope's son, Henry, later edited Bianconi's daughter's biography of her father.

26. 4. Fanny Trollope, who had been quite friendly to the Irish in her book of American travels, became increasingly concerned about sectarian violence in Ireland. See her novel, *The Vicar of Wexhill*, published in 1837.

27. 5. Trollope was born in Keppel Street in 1815.

37. 6. Trollope started his life-long love of fox-hunting in Ireland.

41. 7. Trollope returned to England in 1859 and settled at Waltham Cross in Hertfordshire.

La Mère Bauche

48. 8. Campan is a good example of how Trollope frequently took names from history. Madame Campan was the author of memoirs about Marie Antoinette; Trollope's third novel, *La Vendée* (1850) had been set in the French Revolution.

Journey to Panama

77. 9. On December 20, 1860 South Carolina exercised her right to secede from the American Union. For the next month, until the formation of the Confederacy, South Carolina used a flag bearing the palmetto tree as her banner.

Page 83.   10. This is an example of how Trollope's hurried writing could at times cause difficulty: Amelia was the same person as Miss Grumpy. There presumably should be a "Mrs" where "Miss" is used. The text used in this collection follows Trollope's text in *Lotta Schmidt* (1867).

87.   11. Trollope has the same comments on St Thomas in his travel book, *The West Indies and the Spanish Main* (1859).

91.   12. "Aspinwall" was the name given to this town by travellers from the United States. Trollope, unlike most English visitors, preferred the American usage to the local usage, "Colón".

Miss Ophelia Gledd

102.   13. "If any one were asked to give an Americanism without a moment's delay, he would be more likely than not to mention I guess." (H. W. and F. G. Fowler, *The King's English* (Oxford, 3rd. ed., 1934), p. 33.) Trollope often has his American characters using the phrase; in another short story, "The Courtship of Susan Bell", which is set in New York, it is done to excess. For his use of it in novels see John W. Clark, *The Language and Style of Anthony Trollope* (1975), pp. 121–2.

104.   14. "Britisher" was a common term in nineteenth century America. Trollope is one of the few English authors of the time to use it in his own writings. See, for example, his letters on Ceylon in Bradford Booth (ed), *Anthony Trollope: The Tireless Traveller* (Berkeley, California, 1978), p. 49.

111.   15. Aspasia was an Athenian woman who was said to have influenced Socrates.

115.   16. The decline of duelling is a frequent theme in Trollope's novels, e.g. *The Small House at Allington* (1864) and *Ayala's Angel* (1881).

Charles Dickens

120.   17. After Thackeray's death in December, 1863, Trollope wrote a short tribute for the February issue of *The Cornhill Magazine*, which Thackeray had edited.

120.   18. Both Trollope and Dickens took a strong and outspoken interest in the fact that American publishers rarely paid any copyright fees to English authors whose works they pirated. Trollope had been sent on an unoffi-

cial government mission to America on the subject. Dickens had spoken at the Royal Academy dinner on May 2, 1870. He died on June 8 and was buried in Westminster Abbey.

Page 122. 19. *Dennis Duval* was the novel Thackeray left unfinished at his death. It was published in *The Cornhill Magazine* in 1864.

122. 20. Charles Lever was a well known Irish novelist. On Trollope's friendship for him see Escott, *Trollope*, pp. 50, 167.

124. 21. Captain Bobadill is a character in Ben Jonson's *Every Man in his Humour*; Squire Western is in Henry Fielding's *Tom Jones*; the Vicar of Wakefield is from Oliver Goldsmith's novel of the same name; Colonel Newcome comes from Thackeray's *The Newcomes*. Trollope frequently mis-spells characters from fiction.

125. 22. Dickens satirised government departments in *Little Dorritt* as the "circumlocution office". This infuriated Trollope who tried to write a hostile article about it. See Hall (ed), *Letters*, I. 43–4, and Bradford Booth, "Trollope and *Little Dorritt*" in *Trollopian* (March, 1948), pp. 237–40. Dickens also disliked politicians and was surprised that Trollope made an unsuccessful attempt to become an M.P. in 1868.

126. 23. Earl Russell, Liberal Prime Minister, was a long time supporter of the idea of life peerages. In 1868, Trollope had an interview with Russell and it is possible that they may discussed the idea of life peerages for some literary men.

A Walk in a Wood

129. 24. In *Orley Farm* (1862), Lady Mason forges her husband's will. The plot of *The Eustace Diamonds* (1872) centres on whether Lady Eustace steals the diamonds belonging to her late husband's family. Trollope overheard two clerymen at the Athenaeum saying that Mrs Proudie, the Bishop's wife, had been in too many of his novels. Trollope announced "I will go home and kill her before the week is over" which he did in *The Last Chronicle of Barset* (1867). See his *Autobiography*, pp. 274–6.

Page 130. 25. At the time this was written, Trollope lived in Montagu Square in London.

132. 26. Trollope's proof copy of this essay, in the Robert H. Taylor Collection at Princeton, shows that one of the few changes he made in this essay was to change the statement that it was "hard" to reject a dog's companionship to the statement that it was "best" to do so on a walk of contemplation. I am grateful to Mr Robert Taylor for his kindness in allowing me to examine his collection of Trollope manuscripts.

Editorial Note: In this edition, Trollope's usages and spellings have been retained except in a few cases where confusion might be caused. Thus spellings such as "exigeant" and "chesnut" are retained but an incorrect accent mark on the i in the Pic du Midi has been removed.